Potent nightcap

"What do you think you are doing?" She hardly recognized her own voice.

"Taking off my clothes." His eyes slid insolently the length of her sheet-veiled body. "Don't you undress before you go to bed, *carinha?*" The look, as well as the tone of the voice, told her that he knew the answer to that already. The damned sheet *clung.*

Charlie made herself meet his glance firmly and directly. "Then I'd prefer you to continue undressing in your own room."

"This is my room."

He shrugged off his shirt and tossed it to the floor. He grinned at her, and ran his fingers with calculating delicacy along the top hem of the sheet, just not touching her bare skin. "It has been an amusing game, in its way, but now I require a different kind of entertainment from you."

SARA CRAVEN probably had the ideal upbringing for a budding writer. She grew up by the seaside in a house crammed with books, a box of old clothes to dress up in and a swing outside in a walled garden. She produced the opening of her first book at age five and is eternally grateful to her mother for having kept a straight face. Now she has more than twenty-five novels to her credit. The author is married and has two children.

Books by Sara Craven

HARLEQUIN PRESENTS

Don't miss any of our special offers. Write to us at the following address for information on our newest releases.

Harlequin Reader Service
P.O. Box 1397, Buffalo, NY 14240
Canadian address: P.O. Box 603,
Fort Erie, Ont. L2A 5X3

SARA CRAVEN

Dark Ransom

Harlequin Books

TORONTO • NEW YORK • LONDON
AMSTERDAM • PARIS • SYDNEY • HAMBURG
STOCKHOLM • ATHENS • TOKYO • MILAN
MADRID • WARSAW • BUDAPEST • AUCKLAND

Harlequin Presents first edition April 1993
ISBN 0-373-11549-0

Original hardcover edition published in 1992
by Mills & Boon Limited

DARK RANSOM

CHAPTER ONE

'EXCUSE me, I wonder if you'd do me a favour...'

Charlie Graham's lips parted in a soundless gasp of disbelief and her hands clenched on the rail of the boat until her knuckles turned white.

She went on staring down into the brown waters of the river, hoping against hope that the tentative remark might have been addressed to someone else—anyone else—but knowing at the same time that it wasn't possible. Because there was only one other European on the boat with her—the blonde girl who'd boarded at Manaus.

I've come thousands of miles across the world, she thought, for some peace and quiet. To get away from appeals like that. Yet here—even here...

'Excuse me,' the voice insisted, and Charlie turned unsmilingly.

'Yes?'

'I was wondering...' The other girl beamed ingratiatingly at her as she fished into her shoulder-bag and produced an envelope. 'Could you deliver this for me to the hotel in Mariasanta?'

On the surface it seemed a harmless enough request, but Charlie's interest was aroused just the same, especially as the newcomer, whose name she knew from the scrappy passenger list was Fay Preston, had stayed aloof, barely addressing one remark to her until now.

She said, 'Why don't you deliver it yourself? We'll be arriving in Mariasanta the day after tomorrow.'

'I'm not going that far,' the girl said shortly. 'I'm getting off at the fuel stop, and catching the next boat back to Manaus.' She shuddered dramatically. 'I've had Brazil and the mighty Amazon river right up to here.' She gestured, giving an awkward little laugh. 'I mean—have you seen what they call first-class accommodation on this thing?'

'Why, yes,' Charlie admitted levelly. 'As a matter of fact, I'm occupying some of it.'

Fay Preston tossed her head. 'Well, so am I, but that doesn't mean I have to like it. This whole trip's been a disaster from day one. I just didn't think it would *be* like this—so primitive and awful. I'm getting out now, while I can.'

Charlie looked at her with faint amusement. She had to admit that the other girl looked completely out of place on the unsophisticated *Manoela*. She exuded the high gloss that only money could buy, from her extravagant mane of streaked hair to her designer clothes and elegant sandals. Charlie had wondered more than once why Fay Preston had been attracted to such a holiday in the first place, when she'd have been far more at home on the Riviera or some other expensive European playground.

So she wasn't surprised to learn that four days of drawing water for washing out of the river in a bucket of her own providing had been enough for Fay, not to mention the curtained-off hole in the deck which served as a toilet, and the uninterrupted diet of rice and black beans, eked out by fish and occasional pork if they tied up at an Amerindian settlement.

She said lightly, 'That sounds serious. Have you had secret information that *Manoela*'s about to sink?'

'Oh, no.' The blue eyes seemed suddenly evasive. 'Perhaps I phrased it badly.' She smiled nervously. 'I mean—I just don't want to go any further up-river, otherwise I might miss the return trip.' She proffered the envelope. 'So—if you would be so kind...'

Charlie took it, making little effort to conceal her reluctance. She was being mean, she supposed, but she was fed up with doing favours for people. Of hearing them say confidently, 'Oh, Charlie will do it'—no matter how much inconvenience might be involved.

'Charlie by name, and Charlie by nature. The universal dogsbody,' she'd once heard her sister Sonia say with a giggle, and it still hurt.

She would be going ashore at Mariasanta, so she wasn't really going to be put out at all, yet at the same time she was aware of an inexplicable uneasiness.

She glanced briefly at the superscription on the envelope before tucking it into her own bag. '*Senhor R. da Santana*' it said in a childishly rounded script. No address—not even that of the hotel, although she supposed it was doubtful whether Mariasanta would boast more than one.

Fay's smile was anxious. 'I'd arranged to meet
friends,' she said. 'I thought I'd better drop them
a line—explain why I couldn't make it after all.'

Curiouser and curiouser, Charlie thought, especially as these 'friends' appeared to be male
and in the singular. But what the hell? she called
herself to order. It was really none of her
business.

She said drily, 'So—I just leave this at the hotel
for collection?'

The other nodded eagerly. 'If you wouldn't
mind. I can't thank you enough.'

'It's all right,' Charlie returned with more civ-
ility than truth, and Fay flashed her another
brittle smile before walking off, her heels wob-
bling on the uneven deck, leaving Charlie to
return to her fascinated scrutiny of the passing
scenery.

When she'd begun this cruise the Amazon had
seemed as wide as some vast ocean, but now it
had narrowed, closed in on the *Manoela*, the high
green forest which bordered it seeming almost
accessible—as if she could stretch out her arm
and touch it. Reminding her of one of the reasons
behind this journey. One which she'd barely acknowledged, even to herself, before throwing off
the shackles and restraints of home.

She sighed, remembering the furore when she'd
announced her intention of taking a holiday in
the Brazilian interior.

'You surely aren't serious.' Her mother's face
had been totally outraged. 'What on earth will
you do—miles from civilisation like that?'

Be on my own for once, Charlie had thought fiercely. Enjoy a few weeks of independence.

But she hadn't said so aloud. Like so many selfish and demanding people, her mother had feelings all too easily wounded, and any such remark from Charlie would have been met with days of sulks and pointed remarks. She'd learned to her cost and long ago that it simply wasn't worth it.

Instead she'd said quietly, 'It's always been an ambition of mine.'

'What curious ambitions you do have,' Sonia had drawled, putting down her coffee-cup. 'One minute you're skivvying for a pack of ungrateful old biddies. The next you're vanishing up the Amazon. What will the local geriatric brigade do without you?'

'Oh, don't even talk about it,' Mrs Graham said pettishly. 'It's enough disgrace having a daughter in domestic service, without allowing it to become a topic of conversation in my own sitting-room.'

'I'm a home help,' Charlie said patiently. 'And I happen to like my old ladies very much.'

Sonia gave a silvery laugh. 'Well, you have every reason to adore the late Mrs Hughes, leaving you that weird legacy to be spent on foreign travel. Although I bet she didn't have the Amazon in mind. She probably expected you'd do a guided educational tour round the European capitals and meet some suitable man.' She gave her sister's slight figure a disparaging look. 'But then, of course, she didn't really know you very well, did she?'

'Perhaps not,' Charlie agreed colourlessly. She wondered if by 'suitable' Sonia was thinking of someone like her own husband. In Charlie's view, Gordon was a smug, self-opinionated bore, smart and sleek on the surface, but already running to fat in his designer suits like an over-stuffed sofa. But as Sonia and their mother were totally complacent about the marriage, Charlie kept her opinions carefully to herself.

'So, cleaning all that silver and listening to her endless ramblings paid dividends in the end.' Sonia lit a cigarette. 'Really quite clever of you, sweetie.'

Charlie boiled inwardly, and silently. It hadn't been clever at all. Mrs Hughes had seemed to enjoy her visits, and they'd struck up quite a friendship in the relatively short time available, but that was all there was to it. Charlie had been genuinely grieved when Mrs Hughes had succumbed to a final heart attack, and the subsequent letter from a solicitor informing her of her bequest had left her stunned.

Apart from anything else, Mrs Hughes had lived very modestly. There'd been nothing to suggest she'd had that sort of money at her disposal.

'To my dear young friend Charlotte Graham, so that she may spread her wings abroad at last,' the codicil had stated.

'I can't accept it,' Charlie had said at first, and the solicitor, Mr Beckwith, had smiled understandingly.

'You won't be depriving some deserving relative, my dear young lady. Far from it,' he commented with a certain dryness. 'The rest of the estate goes to Mrs Hughes's nephew Philip, and he, unfortunately, has not been in contact with his aunt for several years. In fact, it isn't certain where he is, or even if he's still alive.' He sighed. 'Rather a self-willed, adventurous young man, I understand.'

'Mrs Hughes thought he was still alive,' Charlie said. 'She was convinced of it. She talked about him a lot—said he'd gone to South America to prospect for gold, swearing he'd come back a millionaire.'

Mr Beckwith tutted. 'A very risky undertaking, and a great grief to his aunt. We shall advertise, of course, but he could be anywhere. South America—so vast.'

In the days that had followed Charlie had found herself thinking more and more about the missing Philip Hughes.

'We quarrelled,' Mrs Hughes had told her sadly. 'I wanted him to continue training for his late father's profession—so worthwhile—and he wanted to see the world. Neither of us was prepared to compromise.' She sighed. 'I, at least, know better now. He wrote a few times from Paraguay, and then from Brazil, but for the last two years—nothing.'

She'd shown Charlie a photograph. Philip Hughes was tall and fair, staring self-consciously at the camera, an arm draped across his aunt's shoulders. There was nothing in his conventional good looks to suggest that underneath there was a wild adventurer yearning for escape.

But then, no one would think that of me either, Charlie thought with a faint grin. Especially when I'm still living at home at twenty-two.

She'd made several attempts to strike out on her own and find a bed-sitter, but each time her mother had reacted with tears and hysterical outbursts about neglect and ingratitude.

Charlie had always hated scenes, and raised, angry voices made her feel physically sick. But some inner voice told her she had to weather the storm about her holiday, or she would never have any personal freedom again.

And when she returned to England, she reasoned, the break would have been made, and she could start, in earnest, to plan a life for herself.

Her grin widened as she imagined her mother's reaction to the fact that Charlie had bought her own hammock and cutlery in Belém for this trip. Mrs Graham, when she went abroad, insisted on every creature comfort known to the mind of man, and then some.

Charlie, on the other hand, intended to travel on the *Manoela* as far as the boat went, and decide what to do next when she got there.

It was odd, she thought, that all her mother's objections to the trip had been rooted in the personal inconvenience to herself. She'd never once referred to the dangers her younger daughter might encounter *en route* in this alien world.

'Probably thinks I'm too dull to worry about,' Charlie told herself philosophically, and, compared with Sonia, for example, she undoubtedly was. Her sister had been the high flier where looks were concerned, and Charlie had existed in her shadow, learning not to resent the astonishment in people's faces when they realised she and Sonia were related.

Now it was wonderful just to be alone, and at no one's beck and call. To be able to stand at this rail, and watch the jungle world of the Amazon passing slowly in front of her.

And somewhere in the depths of all that greenery, on the banks of some hidden tributary, Philip Hughes might be panning for gold.

Now that she was actually here she could admit openly to herself that the idea of finding him had crossed her mind more than once. It might be a stupid romantic dream, but she had the last place-name Mrs Hughes had mentioned firmly fixed in her head. And if by some remote chance she found herself in the vicinity of Laragosa it would do no harm to make some enquiries.

Captain Gomez and some of the crew spoke a smattering of English, but they'd stared in total incomprehension at her hesitant questions.

But that hadn't deterred her, and she planned to make some further enquiries when she went ashore at Mariasanta—and deliver that letter at the same time.

She shook her bobbed hair, smooth and shining as a shower of spring rain, back from her face.

Life might have been something of a non-event so far, but all that was going to change now—and this trip to Brazil was only the start.

Laragosa—here I come, she thought with a swift stab of excitement.

* * *

Her first glimpse of Mariasanta two days later damped her optimism a little. There was a wooden dock, built on piles, and flanked by the usual leaf-thatched Amerindian houses, rising on stilts out of the water. Behind these was a huddle of buildings with corrugated-iron roofs, and beyond them—the rain forest.

Charlie found herself wondering if there would actually be a hotel at all.

She'd had no further contact with Fay Preston, who'd left the boat at yesterday's fuel stop without even the courtesy of a goodbye.

Before Charlie went ashore she took the usual precaution of stowing her passport and few valuables in her shoulder-bag, along with her mug and cutlery, as these items, she'd been warned, might disappear if left on the boat.

As it turned out, finding the hotel was no problem. It was a small wooden building with a sign, faded to illegibility, hanging over the front entrance, and a small veranda, which, like the paintwork, had seen better days. Charlie mounted the rickety steps with care, and went in.

The fan, affixed to the ceiling, kept the heavy, humid air moving, but did nothing to lower the temperature, she thought, wiping her face with a handkerchief as she looked round. She seemed to be in the bar, but the place was deserted. Charlie went over and rapped smartly on the unpolished wooden counter. There was a pause, then a small, fat man in a sleeveless vest and baggy trousers pushed his way through a beaded curtain behind the bar and stood looking at her in silently amazed enquiry.

Charlie said stiltedly, *'Bom dia, senhor. Faia inglês?'*

'Não.'

Well, she supposed it had been too much to hope for, she thought resignedly as she delved for her phrase book.

She produced the letter. *'Tenho uma carta.'* She'd looked that up already. And also how to ask if the recipient was in residence. *'O Senhor da Santana mora aqui?'*

The man's bemused expression deepened, and the shake of his head was a decided negative, but he took the letter from her, first wiping his hand on his trousers, and examined it as if it might bite him.

Charlie was almost relieved that the unknown Senhor da Santana didn't live at the hotel after all. She hadn't relished the prospect of trying to explain in her minimal Portuguese that Fay Preston had chickened out on his family's hospitality. But then Ms Preston hadn't seemed exactly a linguist either, so perhaps the *senhor* spoke a modicum of English.

She shrugged mentally. Well, she'd done all that she'd been asked, and now she could see something of the town before the *Manoela* sailed. It was clearly no use in pursuing any enquiries about Laragosa with the hotel proprietor, but tracing Philip Hughes had only been a silly dream anyway.

She realised the man was gesturing at her, pantomiming a drink, and she hesitated. Judging by what she'd seen on the way, this was the only bar in town, she thought, touching her dry lips with the tip of her tongue, so she might as well take advantage of it, unprepossessing though it was.

'*Agua mineral?*' she asked, adding a precautionary, '*Sem gelo.*'

The man shrugged, clearly contemptuous of anyone who would ask for a drink without ice in such heat. He waved her towards one of the stools at the bar, and uncapped a bottle taken from a primitive refrigerator.

But the glass she was handed, along with the bottle, was surprisingly clean, and the drink tasted magical. Good old Coca Cola, she thought, taking a healthy swig.

The hotel proprietor had vanished back into the domain behind the beaded curtain. Charlie suspected that he was probably steaming open Senhor da Santana's letter at that very moment, and wondered whether it would ever reach its rightful destination. Well, fortunately that wasn't her problem. She was simply the messenger girl.

She glanced at her watch, decided there was time for another Coke, and tapped on the counter with a coin. There was no response, so she knocked again more loudly. The bead curtain stirred, and this time two men entered, both strangers.

More customers, she decided, dismissing a faint uneasiness as they came round the bar to stand beside her.

'*Senhorita.*' It was the smaller and swarthier of the two men who spoke. He was wearing denims and a faded checked shirt, his hair covered by an ancient panama hat which he lifted politely. '*Senhorita*, the boat, he wait.'

'Oh, my God.' Charlie slid off her stool, thrusting a handful of coins on to the bar-top. Either she'd lost all track of time, or her watch must have stopped. Thank heavens Captain Gomez had sent someone to find her. The last thing she wanted was to remain here in Mariasanta, possibly at this hotel, until the *Manoela* came downstream again.

A battered jeep was waiting outside the hotel. The small man opened its door, motioning Charlie on to the bench seat.

Under normal circumstances she wouldn't have dreamed of accepting such a lift, but time was of the essence now, and she scrambled in. However, she was slightly taken aback when the other man, taller, with a melancholy black moustache, climbed in beside her, effectively trapping her between the two of them.

Her uneasiness returned in full force. She began, 'I've changed my mind...' but got no further as the jeep roared into life with a jerk that nearly sent her through its grimy windscreen.

By the time she'd recovered her equilibrium they were heading out of town—in the opposite direction to the dock and *Manoela*, she realised with horror.

Suddenly she was very frightened indeed. She turned to the driver, trying to speak calmly. 'There's been a mistake—*um engano*. Let me out of here, please.'

The driver beamed, revealing several unsightly gaps in his teeth. 'We go boat,' he assured her happily.

'But it's the wrong way,' Charlie protested, but to no avail. The jeep thundered on towards the heavy green of the forest, and if she was going to scream, now was the time, before they got completely out of town. But she wasn't in the least sure that her throat muscles would obey her.

She took a deep breath, trying to think rationally, then reached in her bag for her wallet.

'Money,' she said, tugging notes out of their compartment. 'Money for you—to let me go.' She thrust the cash at the man with the moustache. 'It's all I've got, really.'

The man inspected the cash, nodded with a sad smile, and handed it back.

'I haven't any more,' she tried again desperately. 'I'm not rich.'

Or were all tourists deemed to be millionaires in the face of the poverty she saw around her? Maybe so.

But if they didn't want her money—what did they want? Her mind quailed from the obvious answer.

The road was little more than a track now, and the jeep rocketed along, taking pot-holes and tree roots in its stride. It occurred to Charlie that if and when she emerged from this adventure it would be with a dislocated spine.

The driver was whistling cheerfully through one of the gaps in his teeth, and the sound made her shiver.

He glanced at her and nodded. 'Boat soon.'

She said wearily, 'The bloody boat's in the other direction,' no longer caring whether they understood or not.

The track forked suddenly, and they were plunged deeper into the forest. It was like entering a damp green tunnel. Animal and bird cries echoed raucously above the sound of the engine, and tall ferns and undergrowth scratched at the sides of the vehicle as they sped along.

Charlie had a feeling of total unreality. This couldn't be happening to her, she thought. Presently she would wake up and find herself safely in her hammock on board the *Manoela*. And when she did her first action would be to tear up Fay Preston's letter.

The jeep began to slow, and Charlie saw a dark gleam of water ahead of them. Perhaps there was going to be a miracle after all, she thought incredulously. Maybe this was just a very roundabout way to the dock, and the *Manoela* would be there, waiting for her.

But the age of miracles was definitely past. Journey's end was a makeshift landing stage, at which a small craft with an outboard motor was moored.

The driver nudged Charlie. 'Boat,' he said triumphantly.

'But it's the wrong boat,' she said despairingly. *'Um engano.'*

They looked at each other, and shook their heads as if in pity. Charlie dived for her wallet again.

'Look,' she said rapidly, 'turn the jeep round, and take me back to Mariasanta, and I won't tell a living soul about all this. You can take the money, and there'll be no trouble—I swear it. But—please—just—let me go...'

The driver said, 'Boat now, *senhorita*,' and his voice was firm.

She walked between them to the landing stage. They didn't touch her, or use any form of restraint, and she was tempted to make a run for it—but where?

People, she knew, had walked into the Brazilian jungle and never emerged again. And by the time she managed to make it back to Mariasanta, if she ever did, Captain Gomez would have sailed anyway. He waited for no one.

For the first time in her life she understood why extreme danger often made its victims passive.

You clung to the hope, she thought, that things couldn't possibly be as bad as they seemed—or get any worse—right up to the last minute.

She could always dive into the river, she thought almost detachedly, except that she was a lousy swimmer. And the thought of the shoals of piranha and other horrors which might lurk under the brown water was an equally effective deterrent.

She got into the boat and sat where they indicated, watching as they fussed over the unrolling of a small awning set on poles.

If she was going to a fate worse than death it seemed she was going in comparative comfort.

The motor spluttered into life then settled to a steady throb, and the mooring rope was released.

And as they moved away upstream Charlie heard in the distance, like some evil omen, the long, slow grumble of thunder.

CHAPTER TWO

THE storm struck an hour later. Charlie had been only too aware of its approach—the sullen clouds crowding above the trees, the occasional searing flash followed by the hollow, nerve-jangling boom. But she'd hoped, childishly, that they'd have reached whatever destination they were heading for before its full force hit them.

She'd experienced an Amazon storm her first day on the *Manoela*, but at least there had been adequate shelter. The awning provided no protection at all against the apparently solid sheet of water descending from the sky.

There were other problems too. This was obviously the latest in a series of storms, and the river was badly swollen. The boat was having to battle against a strong, swirling current, as well as avoid the tree branches and other dangerous debris being carried down towards them.

Charlie wondered fatalistically if this was where it was all going to end—on some anonymous Amazon tributary, among total strangers, with her family forever wondering what had happened to her.

Her clothes were plastered to her body, and her brown hair was hanging in rats' tails round her face. She felt numb, but couldn't decide whether this was through cold or fear. Probably both.

Her companions were clearly concerned at the situation, but no more than that, and she supposed she should find this reassuring.

At that moment the boat's bow turned abruptly inshore, and Charlie, blinking through wet lashes, saw another landing stage. They seemed to have arrived.

She was too bedraggled and miserable to worry any more about what was waiting for her. All she wanted was to get out of this...cockleshell before some passing tree trunk ripped its side away or tore off the motor.

Muffled figures were waiting. They were expected, she realised as hands reached out to help her on to shore, and a waterproof cape, voluminous enough to cover her from head to toe, was wrapped round her.

She was hurried away. Swathed in the cape, she had no idea where they were heading, only that she was being half led, half carried up some slope. There were stones under her feet as well as grass, and she stumbled slightly, her soaked canvas shoes slipping on the sodden surface. A respectful voice said, *'Tenho muita pena, senhorita.'*

Did kidnappers really apologise to their victims? she wondered hysterically.

The battering of the rain stopped suddenly, although she could still hear it drumming close at hand. She could hear women's voices—an excited gabble of Portuguese. Her cape was unwrapped, and Charlie looked dazedly into a plump brown face whose smile held surprise as well as welcome.

'*Pequena.*' The woman, tutting, touched Charlie's dripping hair. '*Venha comigo, senhorita.*'

She found herself in a passage lit by oil lamps. She could hear her shoes squelching on a polished wood floor as she walked along. But she was aware of a faint flicker of hope inside her. Her reception made her think that maybe she hadn't been kidnapped but was just the victim of some idiotic and embarrassing misunderstanding. Perhaps these were the friends Fay Preston had planned to join, and this motherly soul, urging her along with little clicks of her tongue, was actually her hostess. If so, she didn't seem particularly miffed that the wrong guest had come in from the rain.

It was an awkward situation, but not impossible to sort out with a little goodwill on both sides, she thought as she was brought to a large bedroom. The furniture was dark and cumbersome, but not out of place in its environment, Charlie thought, casting a yearning glance at the big, high bed with its snowy sheets and pillows as she was hustled past it.

But, when she saw what awaited her in the smaller adjoining room, she drew a sigh of utter relief and contentment. A capacious bath tub with claw feet and amazingly ornate brass taps stood there, filled with water which steamed faintly and invitingly.

The woman pulled forward a small folding screen, vigorously pantomiming that Charlie should undress behind it. Charlie hesitated before complying. She preferred rather more privacy

when she took off her clothes. She could still remember petty humiliations at boarding-school
and on the occasions when she'd had to share a
bedroom with her sister.

'You really are the most horrendous little
prude,' Sonia had accused scornfully more than
once in those unhappy days. 'God knows, you've
little enough to hide anyway.'

So she was grateful for the woman's discreetly
turned back. Thankful, too, to be able to strip
off the sodden clothes from her damp body. Even
her underwear was soaked, she thought as she
wriggled out of it.

She lowered herself into the water with a small,
blissful murmur. The woman sent her a twinkling
glance, gathered all the wet clothes up into a
bundle and vanished with them.

Which was all very well, Charlie thought, but
what the hell was she going to wear while they
were drying? Or had no one yet noticed that their
temporary visitor had no luggage with her?

I'll worry about that when the time comes, she
told herself. In the meantime, the bath was won-
derfully soothing, easing away the aches and tensions of the journey, and reviving her chilled
flesh. Charlie stirred the water with a languid
hand, enjoying the faint scent that rose from it.

Perhaps I'll just stay here, she thought idly.
Until I wrinkle like a prune.

She sighed and closed her eyes, resting her head
against the high back of the tub, while she silently
rehearsed what explanation she could make to
her surprised hosts when the time came.

She was so lost in her reverie that she didn't notice the opening of the bathroom door.

But a man's voice, deep-timbred and amused, saying *'Querida*, were you nearly drowned...?' brought her swiftly and shockingly back to reality.

For an unthinking moment she sat bolt upright, staring at the doorway in blank, paralysed horror, her confused brain registering an impression of height, black hair, and a thin, bronzed face currently registering an astonishment as deep and appalled as her own.

Then she reacted, sliding in panic down into the concealment of the water behind the high sides of the tub.

'Get out.' Her words emerged as a strangled yelp.

'Deus.' No amusement now, only angry disbelief. He tossed the package he was carrying down on to the floor, then walked out, slamming the door behind him.

Charlie stayed where she was for a few moments, until her heartbeat had settled back to something near normal and she'd finally stopped blushing.

Fay Preston's interpretation of 'friends' had indeed been ambiguous, she thought sickly. And the explanation she was planning was going to need considerably more thought than she'd anticipated.

To say that the next few moments promised to be profoundly awkward was an understatement, she thought wretchedly. Merely having to face him again would be an ordeal.

She got slowly out of the tub, and reached for a towel.

The package on the floor had burst open, revealing the contents as a satin robe in a shade of deep amethyst. Charlie shook out the folds, viewing it gloomily. It was sinuous, sexy and obviously expensive. It was also definitely not intended for her, but it was the only thing she had to put on apart from the damp towel, so . . .

Slowly and reluctantly she slid her arms into the sleeves and tied the sash round her slender waist in a double knot. But a brief glance in the big brass-framed mirror on one wall only served to reinforce her misgivings.

It was far too big for her, she thought, rolling up the sleeves and trying to pull the wide, all too revealing lapels further together. She looked like a child dressing up in adult's clothing, and therefore was at a disadvantage before she even began.

She took a last despairing glance, then turned away. It was no use skulking here any longer. She squared her shoulders and walked into the bedroom.

He was standing by the window, staring out through the rain-lashed panes. But, as if some instinct had warned him of her barefooted approach, he turned slowly and looked at her.

Charlie moistened her lips with the tip of her tongue. 'Who—who are you?'

'I think that should be my question, don't you?' His English was accented but good.

Charlie found his tone altogether less acceptable. Nor did she like the dismissive glance which flicked her from head to toe.

She lifted her chin. 'My name is Charlotte Graham.'

'That,' he said softly, 'I already know, *senhorita*.' He lifted his hand, and she saw with a sense of shock that he was holding her passport.

'You've actually been through my bag?' Her voice shook. 'How—how dare you?'

He shrugged almost negligently. 'Oh, I dare. I think I am entitled to know the identity of those I shelter beneath my roof. And now I would like to know why you have so honoured me, *senhorita*. What exactly are you doing here?'

'You've got a nerve to ask that,' Charlie said hotly. 'After your...thugs kidnapped me in Mariasanta.'

His brows snapped together. 'What are you saying?'

'You heard me.' She wished that her voice would stop trembling. 'I was having a drink in the hotel when they...marched in, and told me the boat was waiting. I thought they meant the *Manoela*, so I went with them. When I realised, I—I told them over and over again they were making a mistake, but they took no notice.'

He shook his head. 'Oh, no, *senhorita*. I don't know what game you are playing, but the mistake is yours, I assure you. So—where is Senhorita Preston?'

Charlie bit her lip. 'She—she isn't coming. She's gone back—gone home.'

The bronzed face was impassive, but underneath he was angry. She could sense the violence of temper in him, and shrank from it.

'So,' he said too pleasantly, 'you have come in her place. Do you expect me to be grateful?'

He made no attempt to move, or lay a hand on her, but suddenly, shatteringly, Charlie felt naked under his mocking, contemptuous gaze.

She knew an overwhelming impulse to drag the satin lapels together, cover herself to the throat, but controlled it. She would not, she thought, give him that satisfaction.

She said quietly and coldly, 'You couldn't be more wrong. I haven't come in anyone's place. I only went to the hotel to deliver a letter on Miss Preston's behalf.' She paused. 'I presume that your name is Santana.'

'You are correct.' The dark eyes narrowed. 'Where, then, is this letter?'

Charlie felt faint colour steal into her face. 'I don't know. Still at the hotel, I suppose.'

'What a tragedy,' he said silkily. 'Then I shall never know how the beautiful Fay chose to give me my dismissal.'

She said haltingly, 'I think she found the trip—on the *Manoela*—rather hard to take. Conditions are a bit...primitive.'

His mouth twisted. 'Clearly, *senhorita*, you are made of sterner stuff—contrary to appearances.' He paused. 'Perhaps you will need to be.'

'I'm sure there must be some deep, cryptic meaning in that,' Charlie said wearily. 'But I'm too tired and too upset to work it out just now.

I'm sorry that you're disappointed over Miss Preston's non-arrival, but——'

'I am more than disappointed,' his voice bit. 'I am devastated that my lovely Fay can forget me so easily. We met while I was on leave in the Algarve last year, visiting some of my cousins in Portugal. I was introduced to Fay at a party, and . . . a relationship developed between us.' He gave her a cynical glance. 'I am sure I do not have to go into details.'

'No.' Charlie's colour deepened. 'But this is really none of my business, *senhor*——'

'Riago,' he corrected her. 'Riago da Santana. And I must point out that you made this your business when you chose to intervene. So— eventually, when my leave came to an end and it was time to return to Brazil, Fay told me that she could not bear to be parted from me. She was flatteringly convincing, so I suggested she should join me here for a while, at my expense, *naturalmente.*'

'Oh, of course.' Charlie's voice was hollow. And clearly no expense had been spared, she thought, conscious of the sensuous cling of the satin robe against her skin.

She swallowed. 'Well, I'm sorry, Senhor da Santana, but she's obviously had second thoughts.' She wondered if she should add the civil hope that he was not too much out of pocket but, looking at the short flare of his upper lip and the cleft in his chin, decided that any further comment would be not only superfluous, but positively unwise.

'And so you have come in her place.' He sounded almost reflective as the dark eyes made another disturbing appraisal of her quivering person. 'If you imagine your charms are an adequate substitute for hers, *senhorita*, then you are wrong.'

Nothing had—or could ever have—prepared her for an insult like that. Charlie stared at him mutely, the colour draining out of her face.

She wanted to reach out and claw his face—draw blood, make him suffer—but instead she let her nails curl into the palms of her hands.

She said with brave politeness, 'You seem to be under some kind of misapprehension, *senhor*. No substitution is intended, or will take place. As I've already explained, your men brought me here by mistake and against my will.'

'You fought them?' he asked. 'You kicked and screamed and struggled? I noticed no marks on either of them, I confess, but my mind was elsewhere...'

'No—not exactly.' Charlie bit her lip. 'I—I tried to explain...to reason with them.' She stopped, realising how lame it must sound. She said defeatedly, 'Oh, you wouldn't understand. But you've got to believe that coming here was not my idea, and my only wish now is to leave, and get back to Mariasanta.'

'An admirable aim.' Still that mockery. 'But impossible to gratify, to my infinite regret. There is no way out of here, except by boat, as you came. And while these rains continue the river is too dangerous to navigate.'

Charlie gasped. 'But how long will all this go on?' she demanded frantically. 'I have to get back—to rejoin the *Manoela* on her way downstream.'

Riago da Santana shrugged. 'For as long as it takes, *senhorita*. Until the river falls again you are going nowhere.' His smile seemed to rasp across her sensitive skin. 'In the meantime, you are my honoured guest.'

'But there must be some other way out,' Charlie protested, her whole being flinching from the prospect of having to be beholden to this man, even on a temporary basis. 'I mean, isn't there a helicopter—or something for emergencies?'

'I regret that your presence in my house does not qualify as an emergency, *senhorita*.'

'Well, it does as far as I'm concerned.' Charlie realised she was perilously close to tears, and fought them back determinedly. 'I—I haven't even a change of clothes with me.'

'Of course not. Why should you have?' He sounded impatient. 'But there is no great problem. As you must be aware, I made provision for my... other guest. Feel free to use whatever you need.'

'How generous,' Charlie said stonily. 'But, as you've already implied, Miss Preston and I are hardly the same size—or shape.'

'Rosita, my housekeeper, will be happy to carry out any alterations required.' He sounded bored. 'I will give her the necessary instructions.'

She wanted to fling his instructions, his hospitality, and Fay Preston's entire wardrobe back in his face, screaming loudly while she did so, but she kept silent. She had no idea how long she was going to be here, and if it was to be days rather than hours she could hardly alternate between the cotton trousers and shirt she'd arrived in and this hateful dressing-gown.

Undressing-gown, she amended crossly, hitching the slipping satin back on to a slender shoulder.

'Thank you,' she said tightly.

He inclined his head courteously. 'It is my pleasure, *senhorita*.' There wasn't an atom of conviction in his voice. 'We shall meet at dinner.'

Charlie watched his tall figure walk out of the bedroom, closing the door behind him as he went. Then her legs gave way under her, and she sank down in a welter of amethyst satin on to the elderly rug which was the floor's sole covering.

Under her breath she slowly and painstakingly recited every bad word she had ever known, heard, or imagined, applying each and every one of them to Riago da Santana. Then, at last, she burst into tears.

Charlie had every intention of declaring that she wasn't hungry and of spending the evening alone in her room, but as suppertime approached she found she was getting more and more ravenous. And the savoury smells wafting through the house were also undermining her determination to remain aloof.

Finding something suitable to wear had been a depressing and even humiliating process. Riago da Santana knew exactly what colours and styles would appeal to his former lover, and every item

in the capacious *guarda-roupa* had been chosen
with her taste in mind. They were glamorous and
exciting, with the kind of labels she'd only ever
dreamed about.

'But they are not me,' she muttered as each
garment was brought out for her inspection.

'Não percebo, senhorita.' Rosita's face was becoming increasingly worried as the pile of rejected dresses mounted.

Charlie patted her arm. 'It's not your fault,
Rosita.' Desperately she pointed at a relatively
simply styled cornflower-blue model on top of
the pile. 'Perhaps we can do something with that.'

And perhaps we can't, she added in silent res-
ignation as Rosita pinned, pulled and experi-
mented. Fay Preston had been lushly, even
voluptuously curved. Charlie was on the skinny
side of slender.

Although Riago da Santana's crushing words
still galled her, Charlie's sense of justice forced
her to admit he had a point.

He'd wanted Fay Preston. He'd been expecting Fay Preston. If he genuinely thought that
Charlie had taken her place, with an eye to the
main chance, then he had every reason to feel
aggrieved.

But he couldn't have thought that, Charlie told
herself. Her own lack of experience and sophis-
tication must have been obvious from the first
seconds of their encounter.

No, he didn't think she'd turned up here as his
alternative mistress. He'd just been in a foul
mood, and taken it out on her because she happened to be handy. It was the kind of situation

she should have been used to. After all, she came across it enough at home, and with some of the more cantankerous of her old ladies.

Yet somehow, coming from a man, and a devastatingly attractive man, as she was forced to admit, it seemed more wounding than usual.

She sighed. Men as unpleasant as Riago da Santana deserved to have a hump, crossed eyes—and warts.

Later, trying to find some redeeming feature in the hastily adapted blue dress, she took a long critical look at herself.

Her lack of inches in vital places was only part of the problem, she decided gloomily. She was—ordinary-looking. Not ugly exactly, but nondescript. Sonia had inherited the warm chestnut hair with the glowing auburn lights, and the enormous eyes, dark and velvety as pansies against her creamy skin.

Charlie, on the other hand, had been left with hair that was plain brown and very fine, accepting only the simplest of styles and requiring frequent shampooing. Her eyes were hazel, and her skin was generally pale. Except when she started blushing.

But her appearance really made little difference, she told herself, turning away from the mirror with a shrug. Riago da Santana had made it insultingly clear that she held no attraction for him—and that should have been reassuring.

As, of course, it was, she told herself hastily. And yet... She brought herself swiftly and guiltily to order, and went in search of her dinner.

Riago da Santana was waiting for her in the *sala de jantar*. It was a low-ceilinged, rather dark room, and the long, heavily polished table was clearly designed for a large family.

Charlie saw that a place had been set for her on the right of her host's seat at the head of the table, and groaned inwardly. She would have preferred to sit at the opposite end of that vast table, almost out of sight and out of earshot.

He surveyed the cornflower dress without expression, but Charlie could guess what he was thinking.

He said politely, 'Would you like a drink? A *batida*, perhaps?'

Charlie repressed a shudder, remembering the popular fermented canejuice aperitif she'd been persuaded to try in Belém. On the other hand, some alcohol might get rid of that shaky feeling in the pit of her stomach.

'Could I have a straight whisky, please?'

'Of course.' He was drinking whisky himself, she noticed. She took the glass he handed her and sipped. It was a local brand with a distinctive, pungent flavour that stung at the back of her throat and made her blink a little.

He noticed. 'You are used to single malt, perhaps?'

She wasn't accustomed to spirits at all, as it happened, and returned a non-committal murmur.

The food, when it came, was good—a peppery soup, thick with rice and vegetables, followed by duck in a mouth-tingling herby sauce. Charlie ate so much that she was forced to refuse the rich

chocolate pudding that duly made its appearance, although she accepted a cup of strong
coffee. And that was a mistake, she realised instantly. She should have kept eating. It was im-
polite to talk with one's mouth full, but
conversation over coffee was unavoidable.

He said, 'With your permission, I shall call you
Carlotta. And I hope you will honour me by using
my given name too.'

Charlie stared down at her cup. She said, 'You
must do as you please, of course, *senhor.*'

'You prefer formality?' Amusement quivered
in his voice.

She said shortly, 'I would prefer to be
elsewhere.'

'You don't like my house? It has an interesting
history. It was built originally by my great grand-
father at the height of the rubber boom in our
country. Our fortune was founded on the *hévea*—
the rubber tree.'

'Of course,' Charlie said instantly. 'Manaus—
the opera house and all those fantastic mansions.
They were all built by rubber millionaires.'

'Ah, yes,' he said. 'For a while Manaus must
have been the richest city in South America. The
mistake lay in thinking the outside world would
not want a share in such riches.' He paused, and
Charlie shifted uncomfortably, remembering that
it had been British botanists who'd brought the
first rubber tree seedlings out of Brazil to Kew
Gardens, and ultimately to Malaysia.

He went on levelly, 'While the industry de-
clined, my family's concern for the house and
the plantation dwindled also, as they diversified

their interests into other fields. They were not alone in that. Many similar homes have been allowed to die—to go back to the jungle. I decided that should not happen here.'

'It's certainly very impressive.' Charlie glanced around her. 'Have you lived here long?' She sounded very prim and English, she thought with irritation. In a minute she'd be discussing the weather.

There was another silence, then he said, 'A year—two years. It suits me to spend this part of my life here.' His eyes didn't leave her face. 'And you, Carlotta. Why did you come to Brazil?'

She supposed the simple answer to that was 'for adventure', but she'd already had far more of that than she could handle, so she hesitated.

She said slowly, 'I suppose you could say... I came to find someone.'

'A man?' He drew a pack of cheroots from the breast pocket of his shirt and lit one from the branched candlestick that illuminated the table.

Charlie was taken aback. She'd really meant herself, but there was a slight truth in what he'd said.

'I don't think that concerns you.'

'Then I have my answer.'

'I don't see why you needed to ask the question,' Charlie said with a slight snap.

His brows lifted. 'You are staying in my house,' he pointed out with deceptive mildness. 'Am I not, then, permitted a certain curiosity about you?'

'As our acquaintance will be short, probably not.'

'Sometimes when the storms are bad we are trapped here for weeks,' he said softly, and laughed at her alarmed expression.

She said crossly, 'My entire holiday has been spoiled, and you think it's funny.'

'I am not altogether amused.' He drew on his cheroot. 'As for the ruin of your vacation—well, I shall have to try and make that up to you in some way.'

'Please don't put yourself to any further trouble,' Charlie said dispiritedly. She had more or less abandoned hope of seeing the *Manoela* or her luggage again, and thanked her stars that she'd been travelling light. When she got back to Mariasanta, she thought, she would catch any boat that offered to Manaus, and spend the rest of her holiday in the civilised confines of Rio.

'So, in England, Carlotta, where do you live?'

'In the south.' She paused. 'If you must call my by my first name, I'm generally known as Charlie.'

'Charlie?' he repeated. 'But that is a man's name.'

Charlie shrugged. 'Nevertheless, that's what they call me.'

'And who are "they"?'

'My family—friends—the people I work for. Well, not all of them,' she amended with a slight sigh, remembering Mrs Hughes.

'You live in a city?'

'Heavens, no. In quite a small town—what we call a market town.'

'And what is this work you do?'

The Inquisition is alive, well, and living in Brazil, she thought resignedly.

'I look after people,' she said shortly.

His brows lifted. 'It must be very well paid—if you can afford a vacation such as this.'

'This is a once-in-a-lifetime trip,' she said. 'From now on I'll stick to the Greek Islands. I've never been abducted there.'

'You still claim that is what happened.' His smile annoyed her.

'I'm here, aren't I?' she returned with something of a snap.

'Without a doubt.' There was a trace of grimness in his tone. 'So, where did you meet with Fay? In this market town of yours?'

She looked at him in astonishment. 'I met her here in Brazil—on the *Manoela*. She boarded at Manaus. I'd joined the boat at Belém.'

He examined his cheroot as if it fascinated him. 'So, you had never met before, and you were just... travelling companions. Tell me, did you find a great deal to talk about together?'

'Not really,' Charlie said wryly. 'We didn't actually have a great deal in common.'

Fay certainly hadn't been a woman's woman, she thought, and he must know that. On the other hand, perhaps he just needed to talk about her.

She found herself saying awkwardly, 'She was very beautiful. I—I hope you aren't too disappointed...' She hesitated, aware that she was getting into deep water.

He said silkily, 'Are you asking if I was in love with her? The answer is no. Does that set your mind at rest?'

Why should it? Charlie wondered, discreetly smothering a yawn with her hand. His private life was none of her business. She'd just been trying to make conversation.

But now the events of the day, coupled with the meal she had eaten, were beginning to catch up with her, and she felt desperately sleepy.

She drank the rest of her coffee, and pushed back her chair. She said politely, 'I'd like to go to my room now, if you don't mind.' She gave him a strained smile. *'Boa noite.'*

He flicked some ash from the end of his cheroot. *'Até logo, Carlotta.'*

She wasn't familiar with the phrase, but presumed it meant 'sleep well'.

She said, 'I hope so very much,' and forced another smile.

In the bedroom a lamp had been lit beside the bed, and the covers had been turned down. In addition to the mesh screens, shutters had been drawn across the windows.

Charlie thought sadly about her light cotton pyjamas on board the *Manoela*. She'd noticed there were no nightgowns among the froth of silk and lace lingerie that Riago da Santana had provided for his lover.

'Surplus to requirements, I suppose,' she muttered. But, whatever the world did, she just wasn't used to sleeping in the nude. It was just another aggravating aspect of this whole miserable mess, she thought as she slid under the fine linen sheet, determinedly closing her eyes.

Yet she found sleep elusive. The rain seemed to have stopped, but the air was warm and still, as if threatening more storms, and this made her uneasy. She'd pushed away the elaborately embroidered coverlet, wrapping herself in the sheet alone.

'Relax,' she told herself impatiently. 'There's nothing to worry about.'

And, even as she accepted her own reassurance, the door opened and Riago da Santana sauntered into the room.

CHAPTER THREE

PARALYSED, Charlie watched him approach and sit down on the edge of the bed. Riago da Santana was carrying, she noticed, the whisky bottle and two glasses.

He said, 'I've brought you a nightcap, Carlotta. Isn't that the English custom?'

'Yes—I mean, I don't know.' Charlie tried to slide further under the sheet, without making it too obvious. She said, her voice croaking a little, 'I don't really want another drink—thank you, *senhor*.'

'But you won't object if I have one?' He poured out some whisky, and drained the glass with one swift, practised movement of his wrist.

He was, she realised, far from drunk. But he wasn't stone-cold sober either. And, drunk or sober, he spelled trouble that she didn't feel equipped to deal with.

He put the bottle down on the chest beside the bed, and began to unbutton his shirt under her horrified gaze.

'What do you think you're doing?' She hardly recognised her own voice.

'Taking off my clothes.' His eyes slid insolently the length of her sheet-veiled body. 'Don't you undress before you go to bed, *carinha*?' The look, as well as the tone of his voice, told her that he knew the answer to that already. The damned sheet *clung*.

She made herself meet his glance firmly and directly. 'Then I'd prefer you to continue undressing in your own room.'

'This is my room.'

They were the words she'd been dreading, and her stomach lurched in panic. But she tried not to show it. 'Then maybe you'd be good enough to call Rosita, and get her to make me up a bed somewhere else.'

'No, *querida*, I shall not be "good enough".' He gave the words a jeering emphasis. 'You are where you belong, as we both know, although it seems to please you to play the innocent.' He shrugged off his shirt and tossed it to the floor. He grinned at her, and ran his fingers with calculating delicacy along the top hem of the sheet, just not touching her bare skin. 'It has been an amusing game, in its way, but now I require a different kind of entertainment from you.'

She slapped the marauding hand away. 'How dare you?'

Sighing, he began to unbuckle his belt. 'A little modesty can be charming,' he said. 'But too much becomes tedious.' He stripped off his trousers and threw them after the shirt. 'You will find me generous, Carlotta,' he added almost casually. 'But don't imagine a show of reluctance will force up the price I'm prepared to pay.'

For a moment Charlie thought she could hear thunder again, but it was only the beat of her own heart, harsh and erratic, filling her head, filling her mind, making it impossible for her to think coherently, to act...

But she had to—*had to*. She should make a run for it, she thought wildly, but the enveloping sheet was wound round her like the tendrils of some man-eating plant. And, if she could scramble free of it, where could she go, naked and barefoot? She was in the middle of a jungle, miles from any help she could count on.

Somehow, *somehow* she would have to reason with him.

She sounded young and very breathless. '*Senhor*—you're making a terrible mistake. I don't—I'm not...' She gulped some of the hot, languid air and tried again. 'I...just met Fay Preston on the boat. I agreed to deliver a letter, that's all. I—I had no idea...' Her voice faltered as she saw his cynical grin, because that wasn't the exact truth, and she knew it.

He said silkily, 'And you just...happened to ask for me at the hotel—and then you... happened to go with my men? A whole series of mistakes. Is that how it was?'

She nodded desperately. 'Yes. Oh, how can I make you believe me?'

'You cannot,' he said succinctly. 'And this pretence of yours wearies me.' The dark eyes glittered dangerously down at her. 'Especially when there are other...more pleasurable ways of achieving exhaustion, *querida*.' His hands moved to his hips to strip off his remaining covering, and Charlie twisted on to her side, cursing the strangling sheet, closing her eyes almost convulsively. She felt the mattress dip as he came to lie beside her.

She said huskily, 'If you touch me I'll scream.'

'And who is there to hear you—or to care?' Impatience mingled with amusement in his voice. 'I hope you have strong lungs, *carinha*, because I intend to touch every inch of you.'

'Oh, God.' Her voice cracked. 'You don't even want me...'

He laughed. 'Ah, does that rankle with you, my little one? I regret if my reaction was less than tactful when we first met. I promise I am becoming more reconciled to your presence with every moment that passes.'

Strong, deft hands rid her of the encircling sheet and gathered her into his arms.

Charlie's mind and body recoiled from the contact in shocked outrage. Her sole experience of men so far had been a few fumbling kisses at parties, generally from those who'd been unable to get to Sonia and were salving their disappointment. Charlie had put up with them politely, but there had never been any stir in her blood, no chemical reaction with any of them to cause her the slightest regret when they had walked away, as they inevitably had.

All she knew of sex was what she'd learned in school biology lessons. And now, in a few shattering moments, that safe, sheltered world had been destroyed. She was in bed with a man—a stranger, naked in his arms, the hard urgency of his flesh against hers spelling out an imperative message even her innocence could interpret.

Oh, God, this couldn't be happening to her. It couldn't...

Some still, cold voice in her head warned her not to fight him. He was infinitely stronger than she was, the muscles in his shoulders and arms like whipcord. If she struggled then he might respond with violence, and she would be damaged—emotionally, at least—forever.

Whereas if she...let him...

If she closed off her mind, her senses and her emotions—everything that went to make up the real Charlotte Graham—then nothing could really happen to her. She could stop thinking...stop feeling...retreat to some hidden place inside herself and wait until the storm was over.

It was just a meaningless physical act that was going to take place. It couldn't touch her as a person at all.

He said softly, 'How sweet you feel, *querida*. How smooth and cool, like water in a desert.' His hand captured her chin, turning her face up to his, and he kissed her on the mouth, his lips warm and tinglingly sensuous.

For a moment a shiver went through her innermost being which had nothing to do with fear, and she suppressed it ruthlessly, shocked at her own momentary weakness.

He laid a trail of small, light kisses across her cheek to her ear, gently tugging at the soft pink lobe with his teeth.

'You are trembling,' he whispered.

'Is it any wonder?' She tried one last plea. 'I beg you—let me go, please...'

'Do you truly find me so repulsive?' His tone hardened. 'Then close your eyes, *querida*, and think about the benefits instead. The thought of my money should make you more...amenable, if nothing else.'

'I don't want your money.' Her head twisted in desperate negation. 'I don't want anything.'

'Truly?' he jeered. 'What a paragon you must be. Then you can pay me instead, Carlotta. A payment in kind, in return for my hospitality.' His hand stroked her shoulder, then slid down to close with terrifying intimacy on her breast. 'A debt it will give me infinite joy to collect,' he added softly.

Charlie lay, rigid and unmoving, as he began to caress her.

The ordeal would soon be over, she tried to tell herself. He was hotly, eagerly aroused, and he'd probably been leading a celibate life in this wilderness for some time. She wouldn't have to endure this lingering exploration of her body for too long.

But, as the long, suffering moments passed, she realised she was being naïvely optimistic. For Riago da Santana was in no hurry at all. His hands and mouth touched her as if every cell, every nerve-ending in her quivering flesh was a unique and fascinating experience for him.

He was, she realised, the breath catching in her throat, hell-bent on forcing her to his own pitch of excitement. No doubt her reluctance, her attempted rejection of him, had piqued his male arrogance, and now he was determined to make her respond to him as he wanted.

But it would take far more than determination, Charlie thought, her body jarring in shock as she felt his tongue lazily encircling her nipple.

In fact, she hadn't really the slightest idea what it would take, but it certainly wasn't the kind of practised caresses that Fay Preston had undoubtedly enjoyed.

I'm not even a person to him, she thought, stiffening in hostility as his long-fingered hand slid down to the curve of her hip, lingering there, alerting her to the possibility of other, even more startling intimacies. Just a substitute.

As he parted her thighs she had to sink her teeth into her lower lip, her whole body tensing in outrage.

'You are not a very ardent lover.' Riago da Santana's voice held amusement, and something else, less easy to analyse. He was probably annoyed that his technique wasn't having the desired effect for once.

'I made no promises,' she retorted flatly.

'No, that is true.' His hands framed her face, forcing her to meet his direct gaze. 'But I made one to myself.'

So, she was right, she thought.

She lifted one shoulder in a shrug. 'I'm sorry if it's dented your macho pride to discover you're not instantly desirable to every woman you meet.'

'I do not,' he said with faint irony, 'meet a great many.'

For a moment she was assailed by something like compassion. He'd been anticipating a passionate reunion with Fay Preston, who

probably knew everything there was to know
about pleasing a man. And instead...

She stopped abruptly, right there. Life was full
of disappointments, and he had no right—no
right at all—to jump to the insulting conclusion
that she was on offer in place of the absent Fay.

'In any case, *carinha*——' the mockery was
back in full force '—you should not have issued
the invitation if you did not intend me to accept.'

What invitation? she asked herself wildly. Her
lips parted in angry denial, but he silenced her
once more with his mouth. The kiss was deeper
this time, his lips and tongue exploring her slowly
and languorously, as if he was savouring her in
some intense and unique way. Another quiver of
mingled fear and excitement rippled through her.
She'd never known a kiss could be like this—
never imagined that a man's mouth could be so
cool on hers, so gentle, and yet burn her down
to her very soul.

In spite of herself, she could feel a small coil
of heated pleasure beginning to unwind deep
inside her body. The movement of his mouth on
hers, the play of his hands on her skin were too
beguiling, too insidious. She could feel the resistance, the anger ebbing out of her, and, in its
place—what? Something she could not recognise—or had never before experienced. Sexual
curiosity, perhaps, or something deeper, and infinitely more dangerous. She didn't know, and it
scared her.

Riago lifted his head, and looked down at her.
'*Querida,*' he whispered, 'don't I please you—
just a little?'

It was the last thing she'd expected to hear from him. He was the arrogant ravager that she needed to hate, and now, instead ...

'I—I don't know.' She almost croaked the words.

'Say my name.'

Her throat felt dry. She didn't want to say it. It was too personal—too intimate. It brought him too close, not just physically, but spiritually in some strange way, and she didn't want that. It would be, in its way, a form of submission.

'Say my name,' he urged again huskily. 'And kiss me—just once, *carinha*.'

She needed to say no, to reject him utterly and finally, but somehow her mouth wouldn't frame the word. Instead, on a soft sigh, conjured up from the depths of her being, she heard herself whisper, 'Riago,' and her hands lifted to his shoulders to draw him down to her.

As her lips touched his she knew she was lost. Small rivers of fire were suddenly running through her veins, and her pulses were going crazy. Resentment, bitterness, even fear were being submerged by darker, more potent forces that were impossible to resist—even if she'd wanted to. It wasn't just a kiss—it was a fever, a delirium, a madness.

Somewhere in the hot and swirling darkness that enveloped her she was aware of his hands sliding under her hips, lifting her to the first unequivocal thrust of his manhood.

There was a pain so sharp that the darkness was rent with jagged lights, and she had to fight to subdue a small moan. One side of her mind wanted to beg him to stop. But as she lay beneath him, numb and speechless, she felt her body gradually coming to terms with this new and shattering sensation.

If there had been any justice the pain should have killed the need and brought her, with shame, back to her senses, but, as it receded, Charlie found other, even stronger feelings taking its place. As he began to move again imperatively, intensifying his first possession of her, she arched to meet him, bringing a groan of satisfaction from his throat.

Riago kissed her again, hungrily, the slide of his tongue against hers mirroring the movement of his loins, slow now, and deep, and infinitely controlled.

Too controlled, she thought, her body twisting, obeying an instinct she hadn't known she possessed as her hands tightened on his shoulders, absorbing the play of muscle beneath his sweat-dampened skin. How could he be so patient . . . ?

Even as the question formed in her mind, the rhythm of his possession changed suddenly— sharpened, quickened, as if he was trying to reach some hidden core in her, some undiscovered wellspring of feeling. The savage urgency of it caught her up, and carried her down into some deep, dark chasm of the spirit where all coherent thought spun away, and only sensation remained, a sweet agony splintering her—tearing her apart.

She heard him groan huskily in turn, his body convulsing in spasm after ecstatic spasm, then he slumped beside her, burying his face in the pillow, his arm thrown across her, keeping her pinned beside him.

For a while she remained still as her mind tried dazedly to come to terms with what had been happening. But, as sanity returned, it brought shame in its wake, and a frantic, horrified disbelief.

Oh, God, what had she done? she wailed silently. What had she allowed him to do?

She tried to edge away from him, but the imprisoning arm tightened, pulling her against him. He muttered something slurred and husky in his own language, and a few minutes later his even breathing told her that he was asleep.

She lay rigidly, hating his total relaxation...the way his warm breath fanned her shoulder. They could have been sleeping together all their lives, she thought resentfully. The least he could have done was allow her to crawl away somewhere—heal her aching body in solitude.

But the pain he'd inflicted, though real, was the least of her worries. Infinitely more disturbing was the reality of her own capitulation. Why couldn't she have retreated from him—remained immune throughout it all, as she'd intended?

She could never forgive herself for that—and yet she had to. It had happened, but now it was over. What she had to do was carry on with her real life, as if this had just been some nightmare, terrifying at the time, but forgettable, she told herself, biting her lip.

Slowly and carefully she turned her head and stared at him—this total stranger who had just known her more intimately than any other human being. Who'd made her experience feelings and emotions she'd never dreamed existed.

He was...attractive, she acknowledged with deep reluctance, although that didn't excuse anything.

In fact, he was handsome with a strong, almost classic bone-structure.

His hair was thick, and as dark and glossy as a raven's wing, although it needed cutting, and his lashes were almost indecently long. As he slept his mouth curved slightly, as if some dream or recollection was making him smile.

Charlie shivered, then reached out a cautious hand and turned down the lamp. She had seen, she told herself, more than enough. The last thing she wanted was his image imprinted on some memory bank in her mind forever.

The very last thing, she thought, surrendering her mind and body to weary oblivion.

She was back in the boat, but they were making no headway against the current, and the small craft was rocking wildly, crazily. Oh, God, she thought, we're going to capsize. She seemed to be alone, but somewhere a woman's voice was saying, *'Senhorita?'* A voice she dimly recognised.

She opened bleary eyes to find Rosita standing over her, shaking her shoulder vigorously.

For a moment Charlie stared at her, completely disorientated, then the memory of the previous night's events rushed back to assail her in all their appalling detail. After a cautious glance to ascertain that she was alone in the bed she rolled over on to her stomach, burying her face in the pillow with a faint groan.

'Senhorita é tarde.' Rosita gently touched her shoulder again, indicating that she'd placed a cup of coffee on the bedside chest.

Charlie didn't want any coffee. She required no more of Riago da Santana's dearly bought hospitality, she thought, shuddering. Just her clothes, and a boat-ride back to Mariasanta. Although, at the moment, her most pressing need was for some warm water.

Her precious phrase book was nowhere to be seen, so she had to rely on memory.

She moistened her lips with the tip of her tongue. *'Faz favor—de me preparar um banho?'* she managed awkwardly.

Rosita nodded, a stolid expression on her brown face as if she sensed Charlie's embarrassment and was constrained by it too. She produced the amethyst robe and held it out for her to put on.

'Não.' Charlie pointed to the foot of the bed. 'Leave it there—please.'

She lay staring into space while Rosita busied herself in the bathroom. She felt desperately tired. Not surprisingly her night's rest had been fitful, probably because she'd been terrified that Riago da Santana might waken and demand more from her. But he hadn't—and, thankfully, he'd also spared her the humiliation of finding him beside her this morning.

In fact, she hadn't even heard him leave. And now, hopefully, she could wash last night away from her. She hoped she could erase it from her mind just as easily.

She looked at the robe with disfavour. She never wanted it anywhere near her again. It was altogether too potent a reminder of Fay Preston—whose place she'd been forced to take in the most devastating way.

Forced. The word stuck in her throat. Could she really justify it? she asked herself bitterly.

She should have fought. She should have hit him over the head with his own whisky bottle— kneed him in the groin. It had been crazy—cowardly just to...submit like that.

Reason told her that, in the end, her struggles would have made no difference. Riago da Santana would have been too strong. Even now the memory of his sheer physical power made her shiver. He would have prevailed—eventually.

But I would still have had my pride, she thought. Whereas now... Her mind quailed from the remembered reality. She'd become another person—a stranger at the mercy of her own desires. She'd disgraced herself totally.

When Rosita returned to tell her the bath was ready Charlie responded with a vigorous mime, demanding the return of her own clothes. She shook her head when the older woman went to the wardrobe and began offering yet more of the garments that hung there.

No way, she thought grimly. She wanted her own stuff back. Accepting the cornflower dress, even on a temporary loan, had been a big mistake, but there would be no more such errors.

But she was grateful for the bath. As she lay in the water she began to feel refreshed mentally as well as physically. She trickled a handful of water down her face and between her breasts, idly listening to Rosita, who was moving around in the bedroom, talking to someone, presumably another servant, in a high gabble of excitement.

No prizes for guessing what the prime topic of conversation was, she thought, wondering with a grimace how many other girls Rosita had waited on in her master's bedroom.

But when she went back into the room, a towel wrapping her, sarong-like, from armpits to ankles, she was alone. The bed had been freshly made with clean linen, but there was no sign of her clothes yet. Perhaps they would be brought in a minute.

Unless, of course, Riago da Santana had issued orders to the contrary, intending to keep her imprisoned here in his bedroom, in naked subservience. But she didn't really believe that. Not even he would go those lengths—particularly with a girl who was hardly glamorous, either with or without her clothes.

She swung herself on to the bed and lay back against the pillows, reflecting that she might as well be comfortable while she waited.

It wasn't raining today, she noticed. Thick golden sunlight oozed through the half-open shutters and formed a gleaming pool on the polished floor.

She looked round, taking proper stock of her surroundings for the first time, finding herself reluctantly admiring the proportions of the room.

It was odd to find so splendid a house in the rain forest, she thought. As a residence, it wouldn't have been out of place in Manaus itself. She wondered how they'd brought the building materials to this remote place, let alone found the labour.

Or maybe it had just been bewitched—flown from the city, like Aladdin's palace, to the middle of the jungle, by some demon's curse.

If that was the case, she thought grimly, the demon had also come along for the ride. And, come to that, where was Riago da Santana?

She supposed he must be attending to whatever business kept him occupied in this remote corner of Amazonia. Probably white slave trading...

Not that she wanted him around. It was very peaceful here, alone like this in a sunlit room. In fact, the whole house seemed strangely silent, and the air was almost druggingly warm. Her eyelids were beginning to feel as if lead weights had been attached to them, and the bed's welcoming softness was becoming increasingly difficult to resist.

Riago da Santana's bed, she reminded herself, turning her head to look at the other pillow, remembering suddenly the darkness of his hair and skin against the snowy sheet. She shuddered, putting the image firmly from her mind.

At the same time she wondered what he was doing here—an intelligent, educated man, living in the middle of nowhere in all this decaying splendour. It made no sense.

But somehow she couldn't think about it now. She was too comfortable and drowsy for anything to make sense except the need to sleep, and with a sigh she allowed herself to drift away.

She was recalled to awareness by a sharp, acrid smell—the scent of a cheroot, she realised as she opened unwilling eyes.

Riago da Santana was sitting a few feet away from the bed in a high-backed chair, one booted leg crossed almost negligently over the other. His black cotton shirt was open to the waist, revealing far more of his bronzed hair-darkened torso than Charlie wished to be reminded of.

Instinctively her hands moved to ensure that the towel was still firmly and primly in place around her, and she saw his lips tighten as he registered the gesture.

He said quietly and formally, *'Bom dia, senhorita.'* There was no amusement in his face this morning. No triumph, either, and certainly no desire. His expression wasn't that of the conqueror surveying the vanquished, but set—almost grim.

He spoke again. 'Be good enough to tell me once more exactly who you are, and how you came to be here.'

Charlie swallowed. What was this? she wondered. Some new torment he'd devised for her?

She said huskily, 'Is there any point? You still won't believe me.'

The hand holding the cheroot moved impatiently, almost angrily. 'Nevertheless, indulge me,' he ordered brusquely, and as her chin rose he added, *'Faz favor?'*

She bit her lip. She said in a monotone, 'My name is Charlotte Graham. I'm twenty-two years old, and I'm a tourist. I was travelling up-river on a boat called the *Manoela* when I met a girl called Fay Preston, who asked me to deliver a letter addressed to you to the hotel in Mariasanta.' She paused. 'The rest you know,' she added wearily. 'And why do you want me to repeat it over and over again, when you don't believe a word of it?'

He said harshly, 'Because, *senhorita*, your story has omitted one important detail.'

Charlie stared at him. 'I don't think so. I've told you exactly...'

Riago da Santana shook his head. 'What you fail to mention is that—until last night—you were a virgin.'

It was the last thing she'd expected him to say. Colour burned helplessly into her face. 'Is that supposed to make some kind of difference—to change things? It—it didn't seem to...'

He flung down the butt of the cheroot and ground it under his heel. 'Of course it makes a difference, you little fool. It means, God help me, that I was cruelly, criminally wrong about you. You should have told me...'

She said unevenly, 'And that would have stopped you?'

It was his turn to flush. 'Perhaps.' He shrugged angrily. '*Deus*, probably not—how can I tell?' A muscle flickered beside the firm mouth. 'Last night my sole consideration was my own need. It—it closed my eyes to your obvious inexperience.'

'You don't have to remind me,' Charlie said tautly. 'So—what has caused this sudden light to dawn now?'

His jaw hardened. 'Rosita—the bed.' He paused. 'There was blood.'

Her blush spread, consuming her. 'Oh,' she mumbled. 'I—I didn't realise. But I still don't see——'

'Naturally, she could not wait to confront me with the evidence of your innocence—to reproach me with it.'

'How brave of her,' Charlie said bitterly. 'Why should she need to do that?'

'Because, as she rightly claims, I have dishonoured you—spoiled you for the marriage bed.'

Charlie's jaw dropped in incredulity. She didn't know whether to laugh or cry. 'Isn't that rather an old-fashioned viewpoint?' she ventured at last.

'Not to Rosita, I assure you. Her family has served mine for too long,' he said curtly. 'She knows that the fact I have taken you in such a way has grave implications for the honour of the da Santanas that I cannot choose to ignore.' He paused, taking a visible breath. 'When the river falls, a priest from the mission at Laragosa will come down here to marry us.'

CHAPTER FOUR

THERE was a long, shaken silence.

Charlie thought, I'm dreaming. I must be. Everything that's happened is just a nightmare. I'll wake up soon and it will be over. All I have to do is wake up...

Aloud, she said with taut politeness, 'Would you repeat that, please?'

Riago da Santana said impatiently, 'You heard me perfectly well, *senhorita*. I have sent for a priest to marry us.'

Charlie sat bolt upright, clutching at her towel. 'But you can't,' she declared wildly. 'You couldn't have. It's not possible.'

'I would not lie about so serious a matter.'

'Then you're crazy,' she said flatly. 'Utterly mad. And this isn't a house. It's an asylum.' She took a deep breath. 'People do not...*not* marry each other just because...because they've...had sex.'

'Not in your world, perhaps.'

'These are the nineteen-nineties, aren't they— even here?' Charlie flung at him. 'Or are we in some kind of time warp—back in the last century?'

'Such principles may seem absurd to you, *senhorita*, but they are all too real to me, I promise you. I have seduced you, and now I must make reparation in the only way possible.'

61

'Let me get this straight.' Her brain was churning. 'If I'd really been the kind of woman you thought—another Fay Preston, just here for your entertainment—you'd have let me go?'

He nodded. 'Eventually—when I had finished with you.'

'Gee, thanks.' Her voice shook. 'But, because you've inadvertently discovered that you were…the first with me, you're offering to marry me through some misguided sense of chivalry, I presume.' She shook her head. 'Well, it's too late—twenty-four hours too late—to start feeling chivalrous, *senhor*. I wouldn't marry you if you crawled on your knees to me.'

'An unlikely proceeding,' he said coldly.

'Absolutely.' Charlie glared at him. 'So let's drop this ridiculous discussion here and now.'

'There, at least, we are in agreement,' he said. 'There is certainly no more to discuss.'

Charlie's eyes narrowed. His tone was silky, but she wasn't fooled by it. This was no graceful capitulation on his part.

She tried to find another way out.

'If you're worried that I'll make some kind of official complaint about what's happened— accuse you of molesting me—I swear that I won't,' she began. 'I just want to put the whole ghastly episode behind me, and I'm sure you do as well, if you're honest.' She tried a placatory smile. 'So why don't you just give me back my clothes and let me go, and we'll pretend that last night never took place?'

It was his turn to shake his head. 'That, I regret, is impossible.'

'But it needn't be,' she said eagerly. 'Not if we both agree. I'll even put it in writing, if you want...'

His tone roughened impatiently. 'You still do not understand. Last night I also told you the truth, but it seems you did not believe me either.' He paused. 'There is no way out of here, *senhorita*. The river is swollen and dangerous. No one can arrive here or leave by boat. The risk is too great.'

'But for how long?'

He shrugged. 'Who knows? The storms are expected to continue for several days.'

'You don't seem very concerned,' Charlie said indignantly.

'It's part of life here, and we are self-sufficient for that reason.' He gestured negligently. 'Why rage against something that we cannot change?'

'Well, I can't be quite so casual about being stranded in a jungle with a...a rapist,' Charlie flung at him.

His mouth tightened, and a tinge of colour emphasised the severe line of his cheekbones.

'You will learn to speak to me with more respect,' he said curtly.

'I'd prefer not to speak to you at all,' she snapped back.

'And there was no rape,' he continued, icily. 'You have not that poor a memory, Carlotta.'

There was a loaded silence, and Charlie bit her lip. 'All right, I accept that I'm stuck here temporarily, but as soon as the river's navigable again I'm leaving. I refuse to be forced into marrying a total stranger because of some outdated notion

of family honour. This is my life as well, you
know.'

'And perhaps not just yours,' he said grimly.
'Have you thought of that?'

'What do you mean?'

'Do I really have to explain?' he demanded
brusquely. 'You could be pregnant, you little
fool.'

All the breath seemed to leave her body in one
horrified gasp. She managed to choke a strangled,
'No.'

'It's entirely possible, I assure you.' He gave
her an ironic look. 'For a girl who takes pride in
being part of the modern world, you are extra-
ordinarily naïve'

'Well, I'm not even going to consider it as a
possibility,' Charlie said grimly, swallowing down
a knot of panic. 'And, if it has happened, it still
doesn't necessarily mean that I have to marry
you.'

'You think that I would simply let you go—
knowing that you carry my child?' Now he
sounded incredulous. 'That I would allow my son
to be brought up a stranger to me in a foreign
country?'

'Son?' Charlie reared up in outrage. 'What the
hell do you mean—son? It could just as easily
be a girl—although I suppose a daughter
wouldn't fit the macho image you have of
yourself...' She stopped abruptly, appalled as she
realised the path the conversation was taking.
'Oh, God, I don't believe this,' she wailed. 'I
must be as insane as you are. I'm actually ar-

guing with you over the gender of some non-existent child.'

'By the time the river falls we will know for certain whether or not our baby exists.' He spoke quietly, and Charlie felt a shiver run the length of her spine.

Our baby, she thought. Dear God. Three days ago I didn't even know of this man's existence, and now, between us, we might have created another human life.

It was ghastly—it was crazy—but, for all the bravado of her protests, it could have happened. And she would have to live with the consequences.

But, in spite of that, it was the immediate future that was her most pressing concern.

Boats couldn't be the only way out of this place, she told herself. There had to be other means of transport, no matter what he said, although the alternatives might be difficult and dangerous.

She'd read somewhere that another name for the Amazon rain forest was Green Hell, but there were worse forms of hell, she thought grimly, and she was prepared to risk hacking her way through the jungle with a penknife rather than tamely submit to what he was suggesting.

All she needed was four wheels and an engine, and she could be on her way. If she followed the river, sooner or later she would be bound to come to Mariasanta.

But so too might Riago da Santana in pursuit of her, she reminded herself. He'd made his intentions more than clear and was unlikely to let her simply walk out of his life again. And Mariasanta, naturally, would be the first place he'd look.

On the other hand, he'd mentioned there was a mission at Laragosa. That suggested organised religion, stability, and a strict moral code. If she went there and begged for protection and sanctuary they could hardly turn her away.

But she would have to be careful. Every instinct was screaming at her to cut and run as soon as she got her clothes back, but that would be just plain stupid. And if she started asking even casual questions about vehicles he'd be sure to become suspicious.

However distasteful, she'd have to pretend to succumb, to go along with his plans, at the same time keeping alert to the possibility of escape.

'You're very quiet.' His voice cut across her reverie.

'Be glad I'm not having hysterics,' she snapped back. It was important not to become too tractable too soon. A gradual softening in her attitude, however, might flatter his male ego, and put him off his guard.

Only—how many nights like the previous one would she be called on to endure? she thought, her stomach lurching.

'You are not the only one to suffer,' he observed. His face was sombre suddenly, his mouth set harshly. 'I decided some time ago that there was no place for marriage in my life.'

'Then why not leave it like that?' Her voice filled with eagerness. 'You don't have to do this— I promise you. Get me back somehow to

Mariasanta and the *Manoela* and I'll be happy to vanish.'

'And, as I have made clear, that is impossible,' he said. 'Our situation is like a landslide—one small rock sends it rolling, and then it is out of control. Thanks to Rosita, our landslide has already begun.'

'A servant can have that much influence?'

'Unfortunately yes, when she has been a part of one's life since birth.' His tone was dry. 'My mother appointed her originally as my nursemaid. When I no longer needed a nurse she became my mother's spy instead. By this time she will have radioed and told her everything.'

'Your mother's still alive?' She didn't hide her surprise, and his brows lifted in enquiry.

'Why shouldn't she be?'

'Because this house—the way you live—hardly equates with the normal demands of family life. I thought you were... alone in the world.'

'I choose to live as if I were,' he said after a pause. 'But, as well as my mother, I also have a sister.' Another pause. 'And an older brother.'

There was tension in the air. Charlie could feel it as surely as if some invisible cord between them had been suddenly drawn tight.

'You don't see them?' she found herself probing.

'Not for some time.' His tone was flat and discouraged further enquiry.

There was clearly some mystery here, Charlie decided. On the other hand, it could just be that Riago da Santana was the black sheep of his family, and was living in this splendid isolation by popular request.

What a wonderful prospect for a husband, she thought, moving restively. To her annoyance, the towel slipped as she did so, sliding down over her small breasts, and she made a hasty re-adjustment, aware of his swift, flickering glance.

He pushed his chair back and rose to his feet, and she shrank inside, thinking he was going to come across to the bed.

'I'll leave you to rest now, and think over what I have said,' he remarked instead to her relief. 'Perhaps you would let Rosita know when it will be convenient to move my things. She would not wish to disturb you.'

'Move?' Charlie stared at him. 'I don't understand.'

'As my future wife, you are to be treated with all respect.' His smile was sardonic. 'It is...expected. Therefore, until our marriage I shall occupy another room.'

'That's very considerate,' she said tautly. 'But isn't it a little late?'

'Not,' he said cooly, 'in the eyes of my family, or those who work for us. Why cause needless offence?'

'Oh, why indeed?' she said bitterly.

'Besides,' the dark face was expressionless, 'I did not flatter myself that you were eager to share my bed again.'

'I'm not, believe me.' Charlie spoke with clipped emphasis, then paused. 'If the maids are moving your clothes they can return mine at the same time.'

He frowned. 'Do you mean the garments you arrived in? I doubt whether they still exist.'

'You mean you've had them thrown away?' She glared at him. 'My God, I don't believe it...'

'Why not? They were not particularly attractive, or even appropriate.' Riago da Santana shrugged. 'Until I can make other arrangements you may continue to make a choice from those.' He gestured in the direction of the *guarda-roupa*.

'I'll do no such thing.' Charlie sat up furiously, again to the detriment of the towel.

'Then stay as you are.' This time he allowed himself a more leisurely inspection as she struggled to cover herself. He grinned at her, amusement mingling disturbingly with sensuous appraisal. 'After all, Carlotta, dressed or undressed, you are going nowhere.'

He allowed the words to sink in, made her a slight, mocking bow, then strode out of the bedroom, shutting the door behind him.

Going nowhere. It was impossible to relax—let alone think practically and coherently—with that ringing in her head. After an hour she got up, picked the simplest bra and briefs she could find in the frankly exotic collection on offer, and mutinously zipped herself back into the cornflower dress.

She decided to think about the clothes in the *guarda-roupa* as a form of stage costume— something she was forced to assume for the part she had to play.

But she would have to find something altogether more substantial and robust to wear if she was going to make a run for it, she decided uneasily. Strong boots, for instance, were a necessity. Her skin crawled as she thought of all the creeping and scuttling horrors waiting in the undergrowth—insects, spiders and scorpions whose bite or sting could bring death within a few short hours. And she didn't even want to contemplate the snakes.

Oh, God, why did I ever come here? she asked herself frantically. Sonia's gibe about touring the European capitals suddenly sounded like plain common sense.

As soon as she emerged from the bedroom Rosita appeared and swept her kindly but firmly to the dining-room. The scent of coffee hung in the air, and there was freshly baked bread, Charlie saw, and a dish of sliced pineapple and mango. She hadn't felt particularly hungry, but now her mouth was watering, and she found herself attacking the food as if it were the last meal she would ever eat. Rosita poured the coffee and hung around solicitously, pressing Charlie to finish the last crumb of the last crisp roll. Charlie was made to understand she was too thin.

Clearly Rosita was remembering her days as a nursemaid and saw her as her latest charge, she thought with wry amusement.

When she'd finished her meal she was taken on a guided tour of the house. Although Charlie understood little of what was said, Rosita was clearly extolling its virtues, making sure she appreciated her good fortune. And if you liked large, dark rooms with correspondingly large, dark furniture then you certainly were in luck, Charlie remarked inwardly as she looked around.

It was becoming increasingly obvious that she wasn't going to be left on her own, she realised with irritation, wondering if Rosita was acting on Riago's instructions. Perhaps her unwanted fiancé suspected that she wasn't intending to submit meekly to his plans for her future.

One room was an office, and Rosita ushered her into it, palpably swelling with pride. Charlie stared around her at the charts on the wall, the modern desk with its litter of papers and account books, and the big steel filing-cabinet, and wondered what it all meant—and exactly what Riago da Santana did for a living in this corner of nowhere.

Rubber, she thought. He'd said something about this having once been a rubber plantation before the Brazilian industry fell into decay. Maybe he was trying a one-man revival here.

She nodded and smiled at Rosita, pretending to share her obvious enthusiasm. Whatever his involvement, in his nurse's view, at least, the local boy had made good, she told herself ruefully.

As she turned away she noticed that this was where the radio was also kept. Not that it would do her much good. Even if she knew how to work it, there was little chance of anyone responding to her SOS or understanding her predicament.

Except for one person, she remembered with sudden excitement. Philip Hughes had been last heard of at Laragosa. The mission there might have heard of him, know his present whereabouts, and, if so, surely he would help her—a fellow Briton in trouble—especially when she told him about his aunt. It was a flimsy straw of hope, but she grasped at it eagerly. After all, she had nothing else.

The tour over, she was taken to the old-fashioned *sala de estar*, where further coffee awaited on a tray which bore two cups. It seemed the *patrão* was expected, she thought, a knot of sudden nervousness twisting in her stomach.

Although there was nothing to get in a state about, she reminded herself. Riago da Santana had promised her she had nothing further to fear from him, at least until they were married, and, as she hadn't the slightest intention of marrying him, her problems in that context should be over.

Yet the thought of sharing something even as innocuous as a cup of mid-morning coffee with him was still very much an ordeal, and probably would remain so for the duration of her time here.

Every time she was alone with him there were bound to be tensions, she thought, sinking down on to the over-stuffed cushions of the cumbersome cane sofa. One day she would be able to treat everything that had happened in this place, even the events of the previous night, as a bad dream, but not yet.

And not until she could be certain that the bad dream wasn't going to turn into an even worse reality, she reminded herself uneasily, putting a tentative hand on her abdomen.

She could tell herself endlessly that it wasn't possible—that life couldn't play her such a dirty trick, but, whether she was forced to stay or managed to make her escape, something like ten interminable days would have to pass before she could be absolutely sure that her body, once again, belonged to her and her alone.

She sighed silently and reached for the coffee-pot, pausing as a prickle of awareness along her senses alerted her to the fact that she was no longer alone.

She glanced up warily, and saw him lounging in the doorway, watching her, his expression oddly arrested and faintly grim, as if some un-welcome thought had occurred to him.

But then probably it had, she told herself, filling both cups with a faintly unsteady hand. He had no more wish to be married—to spend the rest of his life with a total stranger—than she did herself, and to come home and find her en-sconced in his sitting-room had undoubtedly brought it home to him with stunning force.

After all, a life sentence was a high price to pay for an hour or so of dubious pleasure.

Especially when she wasn't even pretty.

He crossed the room with that easy, lithe stride, and sat down opposite her, taking the cup she handed him.

'Have you spent a pleasant morning?'

'Yes—thank you,' she said stiltedly. 'Rosita has been very kind—showing me the house.'

'What do you think of it?' He reached into the breast pocket of his shirt for his cheroots.

Impressive was the word she'd decided on, so why did she hear herself saying 'I find it gloomy'?

His brows snapped together, and the look he sent her over the flare of the match flame was displeased.

'It has belonged to my family——' he began, and she cut across him swiftly.

'Yes, you told me—at dinner last night. I like a feeling of tradition—I've learned how important links with the past are from my old ladies. But here it's gone too far. It could be beautiful, but it's oppressive, and that's not just because of the surroundings either. It just seems to have been ... left, somehow—as if no one cared.'

'No one has cared for some considerable time,' he said after a pause. 'I was astonished to find the whole place hadn't been devoured by termites when I came here.'

'Why did you come here?'

There was another, longer silence. 'To grow rubber,' he said at last. 'To build a central processing plant for the *caboclos*—the men of the interior who still tap their own trees. To plant more trees of my own.' He sent her a cynical smile. 'To compensate perhaps for the destruction that goes on elsewhere, and restore the balance of nature. Isn't that what the world wants?'

'It's important, certainly,' she admitted. 'But is it what you want?'

The frown returned. 'Why do you ask me that?'

Charlie pushed her hair back, and returned his gaze levelly. 'Because it seemed to me that you were going to give me another reason for being here, then changed your mind.'

His smile was thin. 'You are perceptive, Carlotta.'

'I spend a lot of my time listening to what people don't say.'

'Explain, please?'

'My old ladies, of course. Mrs Jennings, for instance, moans endlessly about all kinds of little trivial aches and pains because she's terrified that there might be something seriously wrong with her and is afraid to ask the doctor. And Mrs Brent is always telling me how well her son is doing, and showing me pictures of his expensive house and gorgeous wife, to disguise the fact that he never comes to see her these days.' She paused. 'There's a lot of that—loneliness.'

'Yet sometimes it is good to be alone.'

'Oh, that's completely different,' she said scornfully. 'That's something you choose— cutting yourself off occasionally so that you can get some serious thinking done about your life— who you are, where you're going. I like that.'

'But you have been lonely sometimes as well?'

Often, she thought, so often—and most of all when I've been at home with Mother and Sonia, when I should have felt close and loved...but haven't...

Her lips parted to tell him so, then she remembered, just in time, who he was, and where they were, and why, and she shrugged instead.

'Like everyone, I suppose.'

He smiled. 'Which, also, is not what you meant to say.' He paused again. 'Who are these old ladies you speak of?'

'My clients, I suppose,' she said. 'I work for a care agency. I told you so last night.' She counted off on her fingers. 'I do shopping for them, and housework, and help them remember to pay bills. Sometimes I take them for little walks too, and just generally keep them company.'

Riago da Santana stared at her. 'And that is how you spend your life?'

'Why shouldn't it be?' she demanded defensively, and he shrugged.

'No reason. In fact, it explains a great deal,' he added drily. 'Except why you chose to come alone to Brazil of all places.'

Charlie lifted her chin. 'Women do travel on their own these days,' she reminded him. 'You didn't supply an escort for Fay Preston, after all.'

'Fay was well able to take care of herself. And she worked for a top travel company in the Algarve, and so spoke good Portuguese.' He paused. 'You let me think you expected me to come to bed with you.'

'I did nothing of the sort.' She slammed her cup back on to the tray, spilling some of its contents. 'How dare you even suggest——?'

'Then why did you agree when I said I would see you later?'

'Is that what you meant?' She was aghast. 'Oh, God, I didn't realise...'

'Do you speak no Portuguese at all, you little fool?'

'I have a phrase book,' she said with dignity. 'I'd been managing quite well—until yesterday.'

'Yesterday was a turning-point in both our lives,' he said drily. He studied the glowing end of his cheroot for a moment. Then, 'Tell me about this man you came to find.'

That was the last thing she was going to do, she thought grimly, especially if Philip Hughes was in the vicinity, and able to help her.

She lifted her chin. 'I think that's my business.'

'But it has also become mine.' He drew on the cheroot, his eyes fixed on her face. 'Clearly he is not your lover.'

Charlie flushed. 'Perhaps we've just . . . lacked the opportunity.' Well, it was an approximation of the truth.

'And that is how it will remain.' There was an autocratic note in his voice. 'My wife does not seek out any other man, no matter how innocent the relationship.'

She said, between gritted teeth, 'But I'm not your wife.'

'Not yet, but then we too lack the opportunity.'

'Opportunity?' Charlie didn't know whether to laugh or cry. 'Twenty-four hours ago you didn't even know of my existence.'

'You regard that as some difficulty.' He gave her a brief smile as he stubbed out the cheroot, and rose. 'We shall have time to become better acquainted before the priest arrives, I promise you.'

'I don't find that particularly reassuring,' she said bitterly.

'*Que pena.*' He walked over to her, took her hand and pulled her to her feet. 'Tell Rosita to prepare another dress for tonight,' he said. 'This one wearies me.'

'*Que pena,*' she mimicked savagely. 'What a pity. Have you any other orders for me?'

'A smile of welcome on my return, perhaps,' he said. 'And this.' He pulled her against him with a swift strength that she, taken off guard, had no power to resist. The hardness of his body and the all too familiar scent of his skin assailed her senses with potent emphasis as his mouth came down on hers in a warm, sensual possession that permitted no resistance or denial.

It was a long kiss, and when it was over she stood in his embrace, dizzy and breathless, her body churning in fright and resentment.

She said huskily, staring down at the rug at her feet, 'You—promised...'

'And I'll keep my word.' He took her chin in his hand, making her look up at him. Although he was smiling a little, his eyes were brilliant, blazing. 'It was only a kiss, Carlotta, and it was just to remind you that, from this moment on, you will think of no other man—only me. You understand?'

'Yes.' The word seemed choked out of her dry throat.

'I hope you do.' He lifted her hand and touched her fingers quite gently to his lips. '*Até logo, carinha*—for the second time.'

She watched him leave, then sat down again rather suddenly on the cane sofa for the very good reason that her legs no longer seemed able to support her.

Her mouth was burning, and her breasts felt tender, crushed as they had been against the harsh wall of his chest.

'You will think of no other man—only me.' The words echoed and re-echoed in her brain, and she shivered suddenly, crossing her arms across her body in an instinctively protective gesture.

Because, it occurred to her, it was a command that could be all too easy—all too dangerously, fatally easy—to obey.

Oh, dear God, she thought. What's happening to me?

CHAPTER FIVE

IT RAINED again during the night. Charlie, wakeful and restless, could hear the relentless drumming on the roof, and decided that it was marginally more of a blessing than a curse.

At least while the storms persisted they would keep the priest from Laragosa at bay, she thought, irritably punching her pillow into shape.

Dinner had been a difficult meal. Her nervousness about the confused state of her emotions had imposed constraints upon the conversation, and they had eaten mainly in silence. As soon as coffee had been drunk, Charlie had used the feeble excuse of a headache to slip away to her room.

Well, Riago da Santana's room, she amended, except that all traces of his presence had now been removed with discreet thoroughness. But what good did that do, when the bed still remained— a potent and forceful reminder of his usage of her?

Just as she'd been unable, last night, to move away from his imprisoning arm, she now found it impossible to escape from her memories.

But she had to do that. She had to close her mind to the past if she was ever to have any peace again. Because there could be no future for her here in this savage wilderness with a stranger.

Although she seemed to be learning more about him all the time, she admitted unwillingly to herself. She'd managed to discover, for instance, why Riago spoke such good English. On leaving school, he'd been at university and business school in both Britain and America, and he'd spent a year in Malaysia, studying the methods of rubber production there.

'Although the conditions that exist there and here on the Rio Tiajos are hardly comparable,' he had supplemented drily. 'It has never been possible to plant rubber trees in neat rows in Brazil. Henry Ford tried to do this in his model plantation Fordlandia, and failed. He did not realise the Amazon imposes its own conditions on those who try to tame it. The *hévea* needs the protection of other trees and foliage or it becomes vulnerable to pests and leaf blight.'

'Can't the pests be eradicated?'

'I doubt whether we could even identify them all, although some progress has been made. But pesticides must be used with care, or other parts of the ecology can be damaged, as you know. So I have made sure that all the new seedlings I have planted over the past eighteen months are well scattered.'

'But won't that mean, eventually, that collecting the rubber will take more time?' Charlie had wrinkled her nose.

'Yes,' he'd said. 'But time is something we have in abundance in the rain forest.'

Well, Charlie thought, staring into the darkness, that might be true for him, but not for her. She couldn't wait to get out of here, and back to reality. All she had to do was find a way.

One idea that presented itself was to persuade him to take her with him to the rubber plantation and the collective processing plant, and that was why she'd tried to evince an intelligent interest in what he'd been telling her.

And it was quite fascinating, she was forced to admit, although he undoubtedly had an uphill struggle on his hands. It was also gratifying that he seemed to possess such sympathy and concern for the environment. He was clearly a more complex personality than she'd first imagined, and would not be too easy to forget.

Determinedly she wrenched her mind back to her plan. She would have to get him to trust her sufficiently to allow her to come and go relatively unsupervised. And that would be a problem because Riago da Santana was no one's fool. He wouldn't be convinced by a sudden pretence of submission.

But she still had her money, after all, intact in her bag, and once she'd established herself as a regular visitor to the plantation maybe it would be possible to bribe one of the *caboclos* to take her to safety.

It all sounded desperately tentative, she acknowledged unhappily, but she had to grab at any passing straw.

The next morning was dry but humid. Mosquito weather, Charlie thought as she took her malaria protection tablets.

To her surprise, Riago was at the table in the *sala de jantar* when she entered. The small, melancholy man standing talking to him she recognised as one of her abductors.

'Planning another kidnap?' she asked as she sat down, reaching for the coffee-pot.

'I regret your humour is lost on Pedrinho,' he said bitingly. 'And the situation we speak about is no laughing matter either. Some of the *caboclos* have reported seeing *garimpeiros* in the locality.'

'What are they?'

'Prospectors looking for gold and precious stones.'

'Aren't people allowed to seek their fortune along the Amazon any more? I thought it was everyone's dream to find El Dorado.'

'A lot of these men are criminals, seeking to smuggle their finds out of Brazil. They have faked passports from Bolivia and Colombia, and are usually armed and violent. If they are operating in our area the *caboclos* are right to be afraid.'

'Oh.' Charlie sipped some coffee reflectively. Now seemed hardly an opportune time to request a guided tour of the plantation, she decided with irritation. She would have to be patient a little longer.

'So what do you do about these people?' she asked at last. 'Organise a man-hunt?'

'No,' he said. 'Any more than I would deliberately kick a sleeping snake. We organise patrols—let them know they have been seen, and so warn them to come no nearer. Living as they do, off the jungle, with no proper food or medical attention, many of them do not survive. Sometimes the forest sends them crazy. Often they kill each other.'

'That's awful.' Charlie grimaced. 'Can't anything be done?'

'How simple you make it sound,' he said softly. 'You come from a small, law-abiding island, and you think you can impose your limitations on the rain forest—the Green Hell, as they call it here. Do you imagine you can police hell as you would your own home town?'

'If you look on it as hell then why do you live here?'

He shrugged. 'There are worse places. And I have a job to do.'

He was still holding something back and she knew it, but decided not to press the point. Whatever secrets his life might hold were no concern of hers. She didn't want to become interested—involved. That was too risky. At the moment she was merely intrigued, she told herself staunchly, but unless she was careful that could develop into a disastrous attraction.

Riago rose from the table with a brief word of apology, and left the room, Pedrinho following in his wake. They'd both certainly looked grim, Charlie mused as she tackled her breakfast. These *garimpeiros* must be a genuine menace.

When she'd finished her meal she hung around irresolutely for a few minutes, wondering where to go and what she was expected to do. She couldn't face another day wandering from room to room like a lost soul.

Reluctantly she went in search of Riago. She found him in his office, and checked in the doorway, startled, when she saw he was loading a gun, something she'd only witnessed up to then on films and television. But watching it happen in real life had none of the drama or glamour of a screenplay, she realised breathlessly. It was threatening and sinister.

Riago looked round, half smiling as he registered her presence in the doorway, but his expression changed when he saw her face.

'Is something wrong?'

'You're not actually going to use that?'

His brows rose in faint hauteur. 'Yes, if I need to. You disapprove?'

'Well, of course I do.' Her hands twisted together. 'I hate any kind of violence.'

'You think you are alone in that?' Riago shook his head. 'But there are situations when ideals will no longer serve—and realism must prevail.' He slid the gun into a holster on his hip. 'Believe me, Carlotta, I will defend myself and what belongs to me. No one takes what I do not want to give.'

'You sound as if we were under siege.'

'Sometimes I feel as if we are.' His voice was suddenly weary. 'Every day there is the eternal battle with the environment here to guard my plantation against insects and blight—to protect my workers against disease and death. There are predators everywhere, and the worst are the human kind.' He paused. 'But I'm sure you did not seek me out just to discuss the evil of violence.'

Charlie bit her lip. 'No. I came to ask how I'm expected to occupy myself here. You have the plantation, and Rosita and the servants look after the house, but I have nothing to do, and it gets tedious.'

'It bores you to learn how to manage my household?'

'I didn't realise that's what I was supposed to be doing,' Charlie said tautly. 'Quite apart from the language barrier, your household seems to manage very well already without my intervention.'

'Rosita is a jewel,' he agreed. 'But until you have learned some Portuguese I shall have to provide you with an interpreter. Rosita's nephew Agenor speaks some English. I'll ask him to come up to the *fazenda*.'

'That would be a start,' Charlie admitted. 'But it's still a very long day.'

He was silent for a moment. 'I brought a crate of books when I came here—some English ones among them,' he said at last. 'I will have them unpacked for you.'

'Thank you,' she said. 'But I can do without *The Do-it-yourself Guide to Latex Production*.'

His lips quirked in faint amusement. 'I think you will find them slightly more entertaining than that. Do you sew? According to my mother, there is always mending to be done.'

'I knew this was a time warp,' she said bitterly. 'What else?'

'You could always pamper yourself a little,' he suggested silkily. 'Make yourself beautiful for my homecoming tonight.'

It was what Fay Preston would have done, she thought, remembering grudgingly the blonde girl's high-gloss exterior and faultlessly enamelled nails. Fay would probably have spent hours bathing and scenting herself, ready for her lover's pleasure.

The thought sent a flare of colour into her cheeks and an edge to her voice.

'I'm afraid that's not my style.'

'You see no need to make yourself desirable for your man?' His eyes flicked over her in sardonic enquiry, and her flush deepened.

'Frankly, no.'

'A pity,' he said. 'But you will learn, and it will be my pleasure to teach you.' His voice was caressing, deliberately seductive, and to her horror Charlie felt a little stir of excitement deep within her in response.

'Don't count on it,' she snapped, then turned on her heel and marched away, hearing his laughter follow her.

She went into the bedroom, slamming the door behind her. She found she was trembling, and this annoyed her even more. She couldn't afford to let him get to her like this, or to remember what it had been like in his arms that night.

She walked over to the *guarda-roupa* and opened the door, glaring at the clothes that hung there as if they were to blame for everything. From now on, she resolved, anything she wore would be hers alone, and not some pathetic adaptation.

When Rosita had shown her round she'd seen a sewing-room with bolts of cloth in it—cotton prints in bright, clear colours. She knew her measurements well enough and had done a certain amount of dressmaking in the past. She could surely make herself some basic, simple shifts, practical but without allure.

She waited until she was sure Riago had left the house before finding her way by trial and error to the sewing-room.

She chose a pretty yellow fabric, spread it on to the floor, and marked out a rough pattern before picking up the scissors. She would just have to improvise, she decided, cutting into the cloth with gritted teeth.

She was fully absorbed in her task, when there was a tap at the door, and Rosita peered in at her, her face astonished.

'*Ai, senhorita!*' she exclaimed protestingly as she realised what Charlie was doing.

Charlie gave her a challenging look. 'Is something the matter?'

Sighing gustily, Rosita gave her to understand that Agenor had arrived. Carrying the roughly pinned dress over her arm, Charlie followed her to the *sala de estar*.

A large wooden crate of books stood in the middle of the floor, and beside it was a boy of about sixteen, bashfully twisting his straw hat in his fingers.

'*Bom dia, senhorita,*' he greeted her. 'The *patrão* has sent me to speak for you.'

'I'm very grateful, Agenor. Perhaps you'll also be able to teach me some Portuguese.' Charlie smiled at him. 'In the meantime, can you ask your aunt to bring me the sewing-machine?'

Rosita appeared displeased by the request. It was, Agenor relayed, her pleasure to alter dresses for the *senhorita*, who should not concern herself with such mundane tasks, and with such plain material.

'I prefer my own style,' Charlie returned coolly, and Rosita, still grumbling, reluctantly subsided.

While the sewing-machine was being brought Charlie began to go through the books in the crate. To her surprise she found some English classic writers, Dickens and Thomas Hardy among them, as well as a selection of popular modern novels. And she was delighted to come across a Wilbur Smith and a Stephen King, neither of which she'd read.

There were some empty shelves in a cupboard at the end of the room, and she arranged the books on these, reserving *Bleak House* for her immediate use. Agenor helped her. His English bordered on the rudimentary, but, with a certain amount of miming and a lot of goodwill, Charlie found they were able to communicate reasonably well.

The sewing-machine turned out to be an old-fashioned hand-operated model. Charlie threaded it, and began machining her seams, chatting to Agenor while she did so.

He was clearly very much in awe of his surroundings, and of the *patrão*, whose name came often into his halting conversation.

Riago da Santana, Charlie realised, startled, was very much revered in the locality. The processing plant which he'd built for the rubber was very modern, Agenor said proudly, and the *patrão* also organised the transportation and sale of the processed latex in Manaus.

News that he had found a bride and was soon to be married had spread like wildfire, and the whole estate was preparing to celebrate the wedding, Agenor added, beaming. Charlie felt like a worm.

She was just debating over the length of her new creation when there was sudden uproar, and Rosita came flying back into the room.

'A man found in forest,' Agenor translated her excited words. 'Hurt bad, very sick—maybe die. *Patrão* says make bed.'

'Is it one of the estate workers?' Charlie got up hurriedly, preparing to follow Rosita.

'No—stranger.'

'Oh.' Charlie gulped slightly. 'One of the *garimpeiros* maybe?' she asked dubiously, remembering what Riago had said about them.

'*Não, senhorita.* Senhor Don Riago would not bring here.' Agenor's chest swelled slightly. 'Besides, I protect you.'

Charlie hid a smile. 'Thank you, Agenor,' she said gently. 'That's very reassuring.'

Rosita was in her element, fetching clean linen for the bed in one of the unused rooms, directing water to be heated, and sending one of her underlings scurrying for the *patrão's* medicine chest.

Charlie was just tucking in the top sheet on the bed, when Riago strode in, the patient carried behind him on a makeshift stretcher.

'Very sick—maybe die.' No one could argue with that, Charlie thought with a kind of fascinated horror mingled with compassion as she watched the man being transferred to the bed. He was thin to the point of emaciation. He was also filthy, an ugly wound oozing sullen blood through the matted hair on the side of his head, and his torn clothing revealed festering sores on his arms and legs.

As she moved forward for a closer look, Riago caught her arm. 'Stand back,' he ordered. 'He has fever.'

'Will he be all right?' Charlie asked, shivering.

'Perhaps,' he said curtly. 'Go now. There is nothing you can do here. I must establish the form this fever takes, and what other injuries he has.'

'You're going to treat him?' she said uncertainly. 'But you're not a doctor.'

'The nearest doctor is at Laragosa—like the nearest priest. I am the *patrão* here. I look after my people. Leave now, please.'

She obeyed reluctantly, turning away with one last look. And, as she did so, the man on the bed stirred, and muttered something.

For a moment Charlie stood totally transfixed, wondering if anyone else had heard it. But it was unlikely. Riago was washing his hands in a basin of water which Rosita had brought him, and Agenor was hovering in the doorway, well out of earshot.

So maybe she was the only person to decipher the hoarse, cracked sound coming from the man's throat as, 'Bastards.'

She closed the door of the *sala de estar* behind her, and leaned against it for a moment.

He's English, she thought. My God, he's English.

She closed her eyes, trying to remember the photograph of Philip Hughes, and if it bore any resemblance to the human wreck who'd just been carried into the house.

He was about the right height, from what she could recall, and his hair could be blond under all that dirt and grease. Otherwise it was impossible to tell.

Don't let it be him, she begged inwardly. Not in that state. I was relying on him to get me out of here and... She stopped suddenly, hating herself for the selfishness of her reactions when the man, whoever he was, could be dying.

It just shows how desperate I am, she told herself appeasingly.

But the sight of him had cured her totally of any wild notions she might have nurtured of making a solo break for freedom through the rain forest.

With a shudder she went reluctantly back to her sewing.

She was just finishing off the hem of her dress when Riago walked in and dropped wearily into the chair opposite.

'How—how is he?' Charlie bit through the thread.

'In the hands of God,' was the laconic answer. 'At the moment he is unconscious.'

'Then you've no idea who he is—how he got in that state?' She tried to sound casual.

'I have several ideas,' Riago said with a touch of grimness. 'When he recovers I shall be asking him some questions.'

'So you think he will get better.'

'He's had the best treatment we can offer, and Rosita is a capable nurse.'

'I could always help her.'

'I doubt that she would allow it.'

'I'm quite competent.' Charlie was indignant.

'Perhaps,' he said. 'But what matters to Rosita is that you are still an unmarried woman. It would shock her to see you performing intimate nursing duties for a strange man.' He paused. 'And I too would prefer you kept your distance from him,' he added.

'For the same narrow-minded and ridiculous reasons?' she challenged furiously. 'I've never heard such nonsense.'

'Nonsense or not,' he said coldly, 'it is my wish that you stay away from his room.'

'You may be the lord and master on this plantation, with everyone jumping each time you speak,' Charlie said hotly, 'but I don't take orders. You don't own me.'

'Not yet,' he said softly. 'But it is only a matter of time before you will take a vow of obedience to me, so why not prepare for this by learning to respect my wishes?'

'Because I've also taken a vow. A vow that no one will ever ride roughshod over me again.' Charlie glared at him. 'I came on this vacation because I was sick and tired of people dictating to me—making me do things I didn't want to.

You may have forgotten, but that's how I got into this present mess.

'I'm not surprised Fay Preston chickened out,' she added recklessly. 'All you want to do is play the tyrant from morning to night. No wonder you were alone here before I was fool enough to come blundering in.'

A muscle moved at the corner of his mouth. His voice was dangerously quiet. 'Guard your tongue, Carlotta.'

'Why?' she demanded. 'What can you do to me that you haven't done already?'

'I advise you not to find out.'

'Threats?' An unsteady little laugh escaped her. 'You've already threatened me with the worst that could possibly happen—the prospect of being married to you. I suppose you couldn't find anyone to court in the normal way,' she added bitterly. 'You couldn't simply fall head over heels in love with someone—and propose. Oh, no. You—you had to kidnap me. Force a proposal on me instead of a ransom demand.' She took a deep breath. 'Well, let me tell you, I'd rather pay any ransom in the world than marry you.'

'Then that is a misfortune for us both,' he said icily, rising to his feet. 'But it changes nothing. You will be my wife, Carlotta.'

He walked to the door, then turned, his face oddly expressionless. 'And I regret that you dislike the manner of my courtship,' he said. 'Once I wooed a girl with flowers and moonlight, and all the love I had to give. I laid my life at her feet—the life of a da Santana.'

'And she rejected all that?' Charlie shook her head in scornful amazement. 'How very short-sighted of her—not wanting to be a da Santana.'

'Not entirely,' he said. 'You see, *carinha*, she married my brother instead. And that is why I shall take care never to make the same mistake again.'

And, as Charlie sat in stunned silence, he bowed to her, and left the room.

CHAPTER SIX

CHARLIE sat for a long time, staring sightlessly ahead of her, Riago's words whirling in her brain.

Whatever she'd expected him to say, she thought, it hadn't been that, although she remembered now that, when he'd mentioned his brother originally, his manner had been ... odd.

Had this girl's rejection of him driven him to this remote and dangerous environment? If so, he must have loved her very much, she thought, a strange feeling of desolation constricting her throat.

'I laid my life at her feet.' That's what he'd said, and how wonderful for a woman to be able to inspire passion like that in such a man. And how tragic that she hadn't returned it. But then, life rarely worked out that neatly, Charlie told herself forlornly.

At the same time she had to remember that, although Riago's experience with his lost love might have made him bitter and wary of serious involvement with women, it certainly hadn't forced him into celibacy. Fay Preston was sufficient evidence of that.

That had been all he really wanted, she thought. A physical relationship with an experienced and willing partner, and no strings attached. And instead ...

Oh, come off it, she adjured herself. You'll be feeling sorry for him in a moment, and you need to save all your sympathy for yourself. You're the one he's going to marry, knowing perfectly well that he'll never give a damn about you.

She looked down at the dress lying in her lap. The seams need pressing, she thought. I'll have to get Agenor to ask one of the maids to do it for me. And I wonder what it would be like to have Riago in love with me—as deeply in love as he was with this girl?

She stopped with a gasp, crunching the material in her hand, wincing as a stray pin stabbed her flesh.

That was where stupid thoughts like that led, she thought as she sucked the bead of blood away. To pain. And not just the transient smart of a pricked finger either, but an agony deep enough to drown your heart and soul.

She tossed the dress impatiently over the arm of the sofa. She'd intended to choose some more material and start another, but suddenly she didn't have the patience any more.

Anyway, it must be lunchtime, she thought, glancing at her watch as she walked to the door, planning to go straight to the *sala de jantar*.

But as she stepped out into the passage she saw Rosita come bustling out of the sick-room, carrying a bowl and spoon on a tray. When her broad back had disappeared down the hallway Charlie slipped over to the partly open door and peeped in.

The room was empty except for the figure on the bed, breathing sterterously.

Charlie trod silently over, and stood looking down on him. He moved and muttered restlessly in delirium, but this time she could not catch the words or guess which language they were spoken in. She still couldn't work out, either, whether the haggard unshaven face on the pillow belonged to Philip Hughes or not. Only time would tell, she thought.

She touched his wrist, felt the fevered heat of his skin, and the shallow pulse.

Please get well, she whispered silently as she turned to leave before Rosita returned and caught her. Please get strong. Because you could be my lifeline out of here, and I need you desperately.

The next few days seemed to fly past. Charlie found, rather to her surprise, that her life was developing some kind of routine. With Agenor's painstaking help, she was now able to play a part in the running of the household. Rosita was fully occupied in nursing the stranger, so Luisa, the cook, came to Charlie to plan the meals each day and receive instructions for the other servants.

As Charlie's first diffidence wore off she found herself almost enjoying her involvement in life at the *fazenda*. Domestic work was what she understood, after all, she told herself, and it fascinated her to see how the household operated in its isolated surroundings.

Although game was hunted in the forest, most of the supplies came from Laragosa, and there was a freezing-shed where meat and other perishables were stored. The electricity for this came from a generator, but, although the current was available in the house, little of it was used there. Oil lamps provided most of the illumination, and wood was burned in the kitchen for cooking and to heat the gigantic copper where the clothes and linen were washed.

When she queried this with Riago he merely shrugged and said it was tradition.

Well, it might seem primitive, but it certainly worked, Charlie thought with amazement, and none of the maids seemed to hanker for the city or the technical benefits of urban life.

It would be very easy to stop missing them herself, she thought, realising with a sense of shock that she'd been at the *fazenda* for almost a week. It would never do to become too accustomed to the life—too settled. Her prime object was still to get away, she reminded herself forcefully.

Relations between Riago and herself had changed diametrically since his revelation about his lost love, she realised. A distance had developed between them, and when they were alone together at mealtimes, or during the endless evenings, there were long silences.

Riago, she thought, was clearly regretting his frankness.

Charlie told herself she should be glad of this. The last thing she wanted, after all, was any further exchange of confidences or, indeed, any kind of intimate companionship between them.

And, of course, there had been no more attempts to kiss her, which was an added bonus.

Charlie had to admit, however, that she had been startled, and even shocked, to discover,

whenever she was alone with Riago, the depth of
her physical awareness of him. She found herself
covertly watching him, her pulses racing, as he
moved round the room or lounged in the chair
opposite, his fingers restlessly drumming on its
arm, while he smoked his cheroots, or drank
seemingly endless supplies of strong black coffee.
Often she caught a brooding expression on his
face, and found the brilliant eyes hooded and
shadowed. But he was rarely completely still, as
if his suppressed energies were constantly demanding an outlet.

It occurred to her that the only time she had
known him completely relaxed was the night
when he'd slept beside her, but that was
altogether too disturbing an image to contemplate, she told herself, hurriedly erasing it from
her consciousness.

In his way he was just as beautiful and as
dangerous as any of the animals who hunted and
mated in the heart of the forest. Sometimes
Charlie woke when the night was at its darkest,
and heard their fierce, unearthly cries away in
the far distance. It was a sobering reminder of
what an outpost of civilisation the *fazenda* really
was, she thought, shivering, and how closely the
jungle stalked its perimeters.

And, just as it was an ongoing battle to keep
the rain forest at bay, so she had to be similarly
on her guard with Riago and this complex unwilling attraction for him that she could no longer
deny.

It was ridiculous—senseless—and she knew it.
He was a stranger to her, a complete enigma in

many ways, and she had every reason to hate him. So it should be easy to keep him at arm's length physically and mentally—to co-exist with him in a kind of cold neutrality until she could make a run for it.

Only, for some inexplicable reason, it wasn't that simple. Charlie told herself it was because for the first time in her life she'd encountered a dynamically attractive man, whose manner, when he chose, could be quite devastatingly charming and seductive.

A more experienced girl would know how to deal with it—or even turn it to her advantage, she thought. But I can't. I feel like... like a twig, caught in the current of that damned river out there, and being whirled downstream to my own destruction.

But that was negative thinking, she scolded herself. She wasn't going to be destroyed. She was going to survive.

It had been established that the sick newcomer in their midst had malaria—and not, Riago had said, one of the more virulent strains either. There had been more to fear from the wound on the stranger's head, he'd added laconically, but would offer no further explanation.

Try as she might, Charlie had been unable to regain access to the sick-room, which Rosita guarded with all the zeal of a prison wardress. Charlie's suggestion, made through Agenor, that she should take turns in sitting with the sick man, or feeding him, had been met with a shocked negative, just as Riago had predicted.

Riago had said that the stranger would have some questions to answer when the fever subsided, Charlie remembered. Somehow she had to ensure that he answered her questions first.

'My aunt is good nurse,' Agenor announced one morning. 'That man not sick now—want food...want shave.'

Charlie's heart thumped in sudden excitement. Riago had already left for the day, and this could be her best opportunity for a private word with the stranger. If she could dislodge Rosita...

She yawned. 'Well, that's marvellous news, especially if it means she can get back to her other work.' She paused, thinking rapidly. 'Manoel was here earlier,' she went on. 'I think his wife may be starting to have her baby, and he wants Rosita to help. Maybe you should tell her.'

It wasn't altogether a lie, she thought, crossing her fingers in the folds of her skirt. Manoel, the plantation foreman, did have a heavily pregnant young wife with a history of miscarriages behind her, and he had indeed called at the *fazenda* that morning, although on an entirely different errand.

Agenor leapt to his feet. 'I go now, *senhorita*.'

A few minutes later Charlie heard Rosita departing towards the kitchen quarters, questioning Agenor shrilly as she did so.

Now's my chance, she thought.

The patient was sitting up in bed, eating soup, when she let herself into the room. He put the spoon down and stared at her in total surprise.

'Who are you?' he asked in Portuguese.

'That's what I want to ask you,' Charlie returned in English. She went to the side of the bed and took a long, hard look at him. Now she was able to recognise the Philip Hughes of his aunt's photographs. His skin had lost that sickly yellow tinge, although he was gaunt and his eyes were still bloodshot. He had been shaved and his hair was clean, the dressing on the side of his head firmly in place. The wound must be hurting him because he winced perceptibly as he turned his head slightly to return her scrutiny.

She said, 'You're Philip Hughes, aren't you?'

There was a pause, then his lips twisted into an apologetic smile. 'You tell me,' he said ruefully. 'Apparently I've taken some kind of knock, which means I can't remember a damned thing. I haven't a clue who I am or what's been happening to me.'

'Oh, no,' Charlie wailed. 'You don't—you can't mean it.'

'I'm afraid I do.' He frowned. 'And, although it's important to me, I can't quite understand why it should matter to you so much.'

'Do you know where you are?'

'I've been told. Apparently this place is the homestead of a rubber plantation, belonging to the guy who's been mopping me up and giving me injections over the past few days.' He paused. 'Only I gather he's Brazilian, and you're obviously English.'

Charlie nodded. 'This is why I needed to talk to you—to make sure. You see, I'm being held here against my will.'

Philip Hughes shifted against his banked-up pillows, his frown deepening. 'You're putting me on.'

'I'm not, I swear it.' Charlie beat a clenched fist into the palm of her other hand. 'You have to believe me. I ended up here completely by accident, and now the owner, Riago da Santana, won't let me leave.'

'Why not?'

'I'd really rather not go into that.' Charlie bit her lip. 'You'll just have to take my word for it—and also for the fact that you really are Philip Hughes.'

He ate another spoonful of soup. 'What makes you think so?'

'I know—knew your aunt. She talked about you—showed me photographs.'

There was a silence, then he said, 'I notice you use the past tense.'

'Yes, I'm afraid so.' Charlie hesitated. 'I—I'm terribly sorry.'

'How did you know her?'

'I worked for this domestic agency in England. She was one of my clients.' Charlie felt sudden tears prickling at the back of her eyes. 'She was a lovely lady, and very kind to me.'

'I don't doubt it,' he said, after another silence. 'But I'm afraid, even if she is—was—my aunt, she's just another gap in my memory. It—it doesn't seem to mean a great deal at all. Nothing does.'

'And yet you can remember Portuguese.'

He looked at her sharply. 'What do you mean?'

'When I came in you asked me who I was,' she pointed out.

'Did I?' He looked thoughtful. 'Well, maybe that's the first chink of light in the darkness, because I haven't understood one word that big woman's been gabbling at me. Luckily, the boss man speaks perfect English, or I'd be totally floundering.'

'Yes, I suppose so.' Disappointment was almost choking her.

'Apparently there's a medical mission at a place called Laragosa,' Philip Hughes went on. 'This Santana guy says they'll bring in a doctor to have a look at me as soon as the river falls sufficiently.'

Charlie winced. 'Did he say how soon that might be?'

Philip Hughes reflected. 'I believe he said *amanhã*—whatever that means.'

'It's the Brazilian word for tomorrow—or any day over the next year or two,' Charlie said bitterly. 'I used to hear it a lot on the journey upriver.' She paused. 'I thought, you see, that you'd be leaving as soon as you were well enough.'

'That's exactly what I want to do, naturally, but they're hardly going to let me wander off, suffering from amnesia.' His smile was boyish and charming. 'Are you that keen to be rid of me?'

'I want to go with you,' she said baldly.

He gave her a startled look. 'Well, I'm flattered, of course, Miss . . . ?'

'Graham,' she supplied. 'Charlotte Graham.'

'OK, so we're introduced, but that doesn't mean we should elope.'

'I don't mean that either,' Charlie said impatiently. 'But I have to get away from here, and you could help me.'

'In ordinary circumstances, perhaps, but as things are...' He spread his hands deprecatingly, then paused, his glance going past Charlie towards the door.

Charlie knew by his expression what she would see when she turned.

Riago was standing in the doorway, hands on hips. He was smiling, but Charlie could see the glitter of anger in his eyes, and her heart lurched unsteadily. How much had he heard? she asked herself.

'Bom dia, senhor,' he said, strolling forward. 'I am glad to know that you clearly feel so much better.' He paused. 'I see also that my *noiva* has introduced herself.'

'Noiva?' Philip Hughes enquired plaintively. 'I don't quite understand...'

'My future wife.' Riago drew Charlie's rigid arm through his. 'Or did she not tell you that?'

'I think she was just getting round to it.' The other man gave them both an uneasy look. 'I—I wish you both every happiness, of course.'

'And I wish you,' Riago said, smiling, 'a full and speedy recovery—and total recall. Unless, of course, the past is unimportant to you,' he added silkily.

'It might be.' Philip Hughes gave a slight laugh. 'But, unfortunately, I have no way of knowing.

It's a damnable position to be in, as I was explaining to Miss Graham.'

'I do not believe she would be in sympathy with you. Carlotta would prefer to blot out the immediate past, I think.' Riago leaned down and removed the lunch tray, placing it on the bedside table. 'And now we will leave you to rest.'

Outside in the hallway he pulled her round to face him. 'Do I speak your language so badly?'

Charlie tried to free herself. 'What do you mean?'

'I told you to keep away from him,' he said harshly. 'And yet I find you in his room. Why?'

'Why didn't you tell me you'd found out he was English?' she countered.

'Because I did not think it mattered.' His mouth was hard. 'Or does sharing a nationality bestow some sacred kinship in your eyes?'

'Naturally I'm interested. And I've never met anyone suffering from amnesia before. I'm sure if I were to talk to him—about home, for instance—I could jog his memory.'

'This is your home now,' Riago said icily. 'And I am equally sure your fellow countryman's memory will return in its own good time—without any intervention from you. This is your final warning, Carlotta. Keep away from him, or I shall be angry with you.'

'I'm shivering in my shoes,' she said defiantly.

Riago muttered something under his breath, and jerked her into his arms. 'There is only one way to deal with you,' he flung at her.

'Let me go.' Her voice emerged as a croak.

'Never.' The bronze face seemed to have been hewn from teak as he bent to her. Charlie closed her eyes. If she could blot him out of her vision she might also be able to erase what he was going to do to her, she thought crazily.

But it was futile—impossible. The heated pressure of his hard body against hers was a reality she could not ignore. And his kiss was deep and totally sensual, draining the moisture from her mouth and the breath from her lungs. His hand sought her breast through the thin fabric of her dress, bringing her nipple to a throbbing peak of shameful excitement under the mastery of his fingers.

Head reeling, Charlie had to cling to his shoulders to stop herself collapsing on to the floor at his feet. The swift inrush of desire, as unwelcome as it was unexpected, was making her whole body pliant, fluid as he held her against him. This time she found she could recognise the power of his arousal without fear, and a sob, raw with need, rose in her throat.

'Do you want me, *carinha*?' The caress of his voice seemed to splinter on her jagged nerve-endings.

Yes, she thought, fiercely. Oh, yes, damn you. And you know it... But the only sound to escape her was a tiny, aching sigh.

Riago pushed her against the wall, his hand tangling in her hair as he brought her mouth to his once more.

Whatever he asked, she thought as his hand smoothed the slight curve of her hip and moved downwards in flagrant demand. Whatever he asked, she would give. Nothing else existed in the world but Riago, and this ecstatic promise of pleasure.

Or nothing they were aware of until a scandalised voice cut across the sensuous spell which enfolded them, and shattered it.

'*Senhor.*' Rosita was standing a few yards away, her brown face a mask of outrage. '*Basta.*'

With a groan Riago let Charlie go, and stepped backwards. Trembling, hot with embarrassment, Charlie stumbled away towards her room as Rosita embarked on a lengthy tirade of shocked expostulation.

Clearly he was no longer the respected *patrão* in the eyes of his former nurse, but someone who'd once again betrayed the family notions of honour, Charlie thought as she closed her door thankfully behind her.

She threw herself across the bed, burying her burning face against the coolness of the linen sheet, pummelling the pillow with clenched fists, raging inwardly, despising herself for her own weakness.

What was happening to her? she asked in silent despair. Weren't things bad enough already without offering herself to him like that—in a passageway where anyone might have seen them? Where someone, in fact, *had* seen them, and thank God it was Rosita, who would scold and then be discreet.

If she hadn't interrupted, Charlie thought, shivering...if she hadn't arrived when she did...he might have been here with me now on this bed. Oh, God, how could I have been such a fool?

It was shattering to realise how near she'd come to complete and utter surrender. She'd never realised she could be capable of such over-whelming sensations, or that her body could be such a traitor.

And all this for a man who'd admitted openly that he loved another woman, and that he would never love again.

But then men did not have to be in love to satisfy their physical appetites, she reminded herself sadly. Riago could take and enjoy all she had to give while remaining emotionally aloof.

Yet, for her, passion without love would de-teriorate into a soulless nightmare. And this was why she had to escape from Riago while she still could—before her heart and mind echoed her body's betrayal.

She stayed where she was for the remainder of the day, and was sorely tempted to ask for dinner to be brought to her there.

But pride demanded that she get up, bathe and change, as she had done each evening so far, when the maid came to knock on her door. Riago must not be allowed to think she was afraid to face him, she told herself with steely determination. She had nearly made a fatal mistake, but there would be no more moments of weakness.

Slowly but surely she was transforming Fay Preston's wardrobe, and the black dress she chose for the evening bore little resemblance to its former self. Now it flattered her slender curves without clinging, and the knee-length skirt showed off her slim legs. The plunging neckline too had been reduced to more discreet proportions.

When she arrived at the *sala de jantar* she found to her astonishment that Philip Hughes was already there, pouring himself a whisky. He was wearing cream cotton trousers and a bronze silk shirt, both of which hung on his thin body.

'Cheers.' He raised his glass to her with exaggerated courtesy. 'You'll have to forgive my appearance, but these are my host's clothes, and he's built on somewhat larger lines.'

'Are you sure you're well enough to get up for meals?' Privately Charlie thought he looked dreadful, pale, haggard and sunken-eyed.

'I'm a bit wobbly, but otherwise fine. And I don't enjoy playing invalid.'

'Is that something you've remembered?'

He shrugged easily. 'Pure instinct, I guess. There are some things about yourself that you just...know.'

And others that shake every preconception you ever had to its foundations, Charlie thought with a little inward sigh.

She said, 'We have to talk.'

Philip flung up a hand in alarm. 'No way, sweetheart. I saw the warning light when your boyfriend interrupted us this afternoon. You didn't mention the fact you were engaged.'

'We're not,' Charlie said shortly. 'He's asked me to marry him. I've refused. End of story.'

'I've got amnesia, darling, not brain damage.' He gave her a brittle smile. 'That isn't the whole truth by any means—not as far as he's con-

cerned, anyway, and you know it. He's hardly
the type to take no for an answer.'

'And what about me?' Charlie demanded bitterly. 'What if no is the only answer there is?'

He shrugged again. 'Go with the flow,
Carlotta. That's my advice. If he's not your idea
of Prince Charming, just sit back and enjoy the
money.'

'That's a disgusting suggestion. I need to get
away from here, and I can't do it alone. I've got
to have help.'

'Well, you won't get it from me,' Philip said
curtly. 'He's a powerful man, darling, and I can't
afford to offend him. I have troubles of my own.'

'But I'm sure I could do something about that,'
she said eagerly. 'Your aunt told me such a lot
about you. I'm sure there'll be something that
will strike a chord...help you to remember...'

'Why? I've only got your word for it that I
had an aunt.' He swallowed the remainder of the
whisky in his glass and turned to pour himself
another.

'But you don't have to believe only me. If you
go back to England you can get proof from her
solicitor. Mrs Hughes left you everything. Well,
almost,' she added conscientiously.

He stared at her. 'What do you mean—
almost?'

'She left me some money too—to be spent on
travelling abroad. That's how I came to be here.
It was supposed to be the journey of a lifetime
up the Amazon.'

He went on staring. 'These trips can't be cheap.
She must have left you a hell of a lot.'

'Yes, I was surprised too,' Charlie admitted ruefully.

'Lucky you,' he said. 'It was a good investment, for here you are, about to be Senhora da Santana, with lots more goodies in the pipeline.'

'But that isn't what I want.'

'Then that's your problem, sweetheart.' His voice was harsh, jarring. 'Because I have no plans to tangle with your intended.'

She felt sick with disappointment, and not just at his refusal. He was so different, so very different from what she'd been led to expect, she thought. There was a weak petulance about his mouth which hadn't been evident in the photograph she'd seen, and his attitude to her plight revealed an unattractively mercenary and grasping side to his nature. Maybe the fact that he'd been Mrs Hughes's only living relative had led the old lady to see him through rose-coloured spectacles, she decided regretfully.

She heard Riago's step in the hallway outside and his voice calling something in Portuguese to one of the servants, and a wave of painful colour suffused her face.

I want to crawl away and hide, she thought desperately, but I've got to stay and face him—I must . . .

Riago strode in, checking slightly when he saw them both, his glance flicking swiftly between them.

'Good evening,' he said politely. 'I apologise for keeping you waiting.' He took Charlie's nerveless hand in his and raised it to his lips. 'But

I think when you hear the reason, *querida*, you will forgive me. I have been talking on the radio to Laragosa.'

Charlie stared at him, her heart beginning to thud harshly and erratically. 'The river...?'

Riago nodded. 'It has fallen at last. So Padre Gaspar will be arriving the day after tomorrow.' He smiled a mocking challenge into her frightened eyes. 'In only a few short hours, *querida*, you and I will be married.'

CHAPTER SEVEN

'WELL?' Riago's tone goaded Charlie as the silence between them lengthened endlessly. 'Have you nothing to say?'

There was a great deal, but she was trembling so much inside and her throat felt so tight that she was afraid to speak.

She had managed to convince herself that it would be weeks rather than days before the Rio Tiajos was navigable again, and that she would have time to make her plans accordingly.

Now she had something less than forty-eight hours in which to accomplish her getaway.

Eventually she said huskily, 'Is—isn't there still some risk?'

Riago nodded. 'Normally they would wait a little longer, but, as an emergency has arisen, they are willing to make the attempt.'

'Emergency?' she echoed bewilderedly.

'Your compatriot's amnesia,' Riago said gently. He turned to Philip Hughes, who seemed equally stunned by the turn of events. 'You will be glad to hear, *amigo*, that qualified medical assistance will accompany Padre Gaspar.' He paused. 'No doubt, if it's necessary, he will refer you in turn to a hospital in Manaus.'

'Oh, I'm sure there's no need for that,' Philip Hughes said quickly. 'Maybe when this headache wears off completely I'll start to remember things.'

'I do not think we should leave such an important matter to chance.' Riago's voice was softer than ever. 'It's a pity you have no idea how that head wound was caused.'

'Perhaps I hit myself on the branch of a tree while I was delirious,' Philip offered.

'Perhaps.' Riago smiled. 'But if I had to make a guess I would say the branch in question was held in someone's hand.'

The other swallowed his whisky in one swift jerky movement of his wrist. 'Are you saying I was attacked? By whom?'

'That is something you'll tell me, perhaps—when your memory returns.'

An ugly flush rose in Philip's face. 'Just what the hell are you implying?'

'Only that there are several questions which will remain unanswered, alas, while your amnesia persists,' Riago said mildly. 'And if I were in your place, and had an enemy who had tried to club me down, I would prefer to know his identity.' He paused, letting the words sink in. 'Now, here comes our dinner. Shall we sit down?'

It was a wretched meal. Charlie found she was pushing the food round her plate while she tried, feverishly, to think, to make some kind of plan. What made it worse was the fact that Riago was watching her, enjoying her discomfiture, she realised angrily. It was little comfort to observe that Philip shared her lack of appetite.

Clearly he couldn't be feeling as well as he claimed, she thought sympathetically. Nor had the news that the doctor was on his way cheered him visibly.

Perhaps he was worrying over how he'd come by the wound on his head, and if it had been obtained as Riago had suggested. All in all, it hadn't been a very tactful theory to present to a sick man.

She'd been waiting all through dinner, too, for Philip to tell Riago that he now knew his own name at least, even if all other details still remained a blank. But, to her amazement, he said nothing. Perhaps he was still sceptical about her identification of him, she thought. He certainly hadn't shown any eagerness to believe her.

Her heart sank when Riago gave orders for coffee to be served in the *sala de estar*, making it clear at the same time that he expected Charlie to be there to pour it, a formality he'd never insisted on before. But then, they'd never had a guest before.

Charlie, who'd hoped to slip off to her room, leaving both men in the dining-room, cursed under her breath.

When she got to the sitting-room she found that Rosita had already brought in the tray. The pot was old-fashioned and cumbersome, and she found it difficult to lift without burning herself as she filled the cups.

Philip followed her into the room and stood watching. 'Nice gear,' he remarked. 'Silver—and a couple of hundred years old, by the look of it.'

'I wouldn't know,' Charlie said shortly. She was beginning to find his preoccupation with money obsessive. She handed him his cup. 'When are you going to tell Riago who you are?'

'I'm not,' he said. 'I'm not going to claim someone's name on the strength of a photograph I haven't even seen, and the say-so of a woman I've only just met. Supposing you've made a mistake?'

'I'm sure I haven't,' Charlie said roundly. 'For one thing, your aunt actually mentioned Laragosa when she was telling me about you. And, although they say everyone has a double, I don't believe yours would turn up in the same region of Amazonia.' She paused. 'I don't understand this. I thought you'd be pleased that I'd recognised you. That you'd be reassured to find out who you are.'

'It's a label, that's all,' he said dismissively. 'And until I know to my own satisfaction that it's the correct label I'd be glad if you said nothing to anyone—especially your autocratic fiancé.' He gave a slight shrug. 'Besides, with a mind that's a complete blank, I find it hard to be pleased about anything,' he added sullenly.

He began to wander round the room, stopping occasionally to pick up a carved wooden figure or pottery bowl, and staring at the few pictures on the walls, most of which were portraits of men dressed in the clothes of bygone eras.

'Presumably those are some of the da Santana ancestors, all busily engaged in robbing the Indians, and grinding the faces of the poor generally,' he commented. 'They've done well for themselves out of it.'

She said quietly, 'Perhaps that's why Riago is trying to give something back by providing the *caboclos* with their own processing plant, and then finding markets for their latex.'

'Let's hear it for the great philanthropist,' Philip jeered. 'I didn't know you were one of his fans—in fact, I got quite the opposite view, but I suppose, now the wedding-day's actually been fixed, you're going to lie back and enjoy it.'

'On the contrary,' she said. 'I still haven't the slightest intention of going through with the marriage. But I can still appreciate what Riago's trying to do here, and the respect the local people feel for him.'

Philip turned, and she had the oddest impression that he was going to say something but had stopped himself at the last minute.

It's as if he knows more about Riago and the da Santana family than he's letting on, she thought. But how can that be possible if he's lost his memory? If...

She knew nothing about amnesia cases, or how easy one would be to fake, but she was beginning to suspect that that was exactly what Philip Hughes was doing. Her affection for his late aunt had prompted her to give him the benefit of the doubt at first, but every moment she spent in his company was increasing her distaste, and making her more and more dubious about him.

This could be why he'd reacted negatively to the idea of medical treatment, she realised with a shock. Because a doctor wouldn't be so easy to fool as they'd been.

If he's faking, she thought uneasily, it must be because he has something to hide. Something serious. But what?

Her sobering train of thought was brought to a halt by the arrival of Riago.

'How silent you both are,' he observed as he closed the door behind him. 'Compatriots in a foreign land—I expected to find you chattering like parrots.'

'We've been talking about your wedding,' Philip said. 'Your lady seems to be suffering from bridal nerves.'

'I am sorry to hear that, but perhaps I have a cure.' Riago crossed to where Charlie was sitting. 'Here, *querida*, a gift for our betrothal.'

Something cold touched her throat, and found a resting place just above the valley of her small breasts. Charlie looked down in astonishment, her lips parting in a silent gasp of wonder. She was looking at a pendant—a single large diamond cut in the shape of a tear. One drop of frozen flame caught on a slender gold chain, she thought, touching it with the tip of an incredulous finger to make sure it was real.

She said, 'Riago—no. I—I can't accept this. It's too valuable.'

'It pleases me to see it against your skin,' he said quietly. 'I wish you to wear it always.' He paused. 'There are other stones, which I will have made into earrings for you—perhaps when our son is born.'

The colour flamed in her face and she pressed her hands to her hot cheeks with an incoherent little murmur of embarrassment, glancing across at Philip Hughes, but he was oblivious, his eyes fixed openly and greedily on the pendant.

'My God,' he said hoarsely at last. 'Where on earth did you find a stone like that?'

'On my land.' There was sudden steel in Riago's voice. 'The *garimpeiros* do not get them all, *amigo*, I promise you. I had it cut in Manaus.'

'Well, whoever it was did an incredible job.' Philip gave an uneven laugh. 'Once in a lifetime you come across something like that. Your wife is a fortunate lady.'

'I hope she shares your opinion,' Riago murmured.

Charlie was lost for words—incapable of rational thought. It wasn't just the value of the gift which she found bewildering, but its timing— and the reasoning behind it. If Riago thought that showering her with diamonds was going to make her any more amenable to being forced into a loveless marriage with him then he was wrong. Surely she'd never given him the impression that she could be bought, she thought wretchedly. If so she would have to disabuse him of the notion, and fast—attempt to make him see one last time that marriage between them was impossible, that it could never work on the terms he was offering.

He should marry for love, she thought painfully, and not because of some outdated idea of family honour. And the girl he marries should become the centre of his world, not some unconsidered trifle on its perimeter. He doesn't deserve to settle for second-best.

But then, neither did she.

And it would be agony beyond words to belong
to him, knowing that she was not, and never
could be, what he really wanted, and that he
would never love her. No diamond in the world
could assuage the hurt of that, she told herself
desolately.

And stopped dead as she realised, with a kind
of fascinated horror, the path her thoughts were
taking.

It's as if I'm in love with him, she realised incredulously. It's as if I want him to be in love
with me. But it's not true. It can't be true—it
can't ...

She must have made some kind of sound, because Riago said sharply, 'What is it? Do you
feel ill?'

Charlie shook her head and got to her feet,
forcing a nervous smile. 'I—I feel rather over-
whelmed, that's all. Perhaps you'll excuse me.'

She was aware of his eyes on her as she made
her way to the door. She made herself walk
without haste, giving no clue to the inner turmoil
laying her emotions waste. She even turned at
the door and smiled again, and lifted her hand
as both men wished her goodnight.

Once in the hallway, uncaring who might see,
she ran like some wild, hunted thing to the safety
of her room.

The bed was turned down, waiting for her.
Moving like an automaton, she undressed and put
on the amethyst robe, now almost a familiar
friend, but she couldn't rest. Instead she extin-
guished the lamp beside the bed and began to

walk up and down, pacing out the length and breadth of the room in the starlit darkness.

She was completely stunned by the revelation that had come to her—could hardly bear to give it credence. But she knew that she must.

She had told herself so loudly and so often that she hated Riago. She had allowed believing in that hatred to become a habit, and had not bothered to examine the ambivalence of her real feelings towards him.

She'd always visualised falling in love with a man as a sweet and steady progression. Safety, she thought, and stability, leading in time to a lifelong commitment. Yet Riago had swept her away with all the power and force of a jungle storm. When he'd taken her body he'd also devastated her mind and senses. She supposed it was inevitable, bearing in mind his attraction and her own inexperience. Even that first night, he'd been able to make her respond to him—and ever since she'd lived on the edge of torment.

I love him, she thought, and I need him to love me—to share his life with me. But it has to be his whole life, not a few fragments of it, spared out of some misplaced sense of duty. And that will never happen.

'I laid my life at her feet.' The words stung at her brain. 'I shall take care never to make the same mistake again.'

He could not have made it more chillingly plain that she had nothing to hope for from him.

She drew a deep, trembling sigh. She couldn't pretend indifference any more when he held her in his arms. She'd betrayed herself too deeply for that already. And sooner or later she would speak the words that must not be said, and give herself away completely.

And that was why she had to leave—to escape from him, however much it might hurt. Because to stay—loving him, yet not having that love returned—would be a kind of slow death.

Instinct told her that that kind of feeling was encountered only once in a lifetime. And the pinnacle of existence would be to have it returned in full.

But I'm too late, she thought sadly. All Riago's passion and commitment were destined for another woman. And now there's nothing left.

I was so afraid I was being kidnapped when I came here, but that would have been the easy option—to hand over money for my ransom and go.

Unrequited love is so much worse—a dark ransom I could go on paying for the rest of my life.

She stood for a moment, staring at the window, where a moth almost as large as the palm of her hand was fluttering against the mesh screen as if trying to gain access.

Then she squared her shoulders, and went out of the room and down the shadowy hallway to the room that Riago was now occupying. She opened the door quietly, and slipped inside.

She thought she'd made no sound, but in an instant he was awake and sitting up in bed.

'*Que quer?*' he demanded harshly. 'What do you want?'

'I need to talk to you.'

There was a silence, then he said more gently, 'You should not be here, Carlotta. It must be late. Go back to your bed, and we will talk in the morning.'

'No, now—please.'

He sighed. She heard him reach for the matches and light the lamp beside the bed. Against the white sheet his skin looked like burnished mahogany.

She moistened dry lips with the tip of her tongue. 'I've come to ask you for the last time to let me go.'

'And you already know my answer.'

She folded her arms across her body. 'Listen to me—I beg you. There was a mistake—a mis-understanding,' she said quietly. 'That's all it was, and we don't have to ruin both our lives because of it.'

'You talk of ruin—I speak of marriage.'

'So do I—for both of us—some time in the future, when we both meet other people we could...love.' The word hurt her throat, but she said it.

'But I have already met the woman I shall love all my life—and she doesn't want me.' His words sounded as bleak as the half-smile which accompanied them, and Charlie felt her heart twist inside her.

'For God's sake, Riago.' She spread her hands in entreaty. 'We can't go through with this...meaningless pretence. Surely you can see that it's impossible?'

'I am pretending nothing.' The dark eyes flashed at her. 'I need a wife at my table, and a

woman in my bed. You...satisfy my requirements. I ask no more than that.'

'Well, I want a great deal more from life,' she
said angrily.

'Yet what life did you have before you came
here?' he demanded. 'On your own admission,
you were hardly more than a servant.'

'I had my independence.' Charlie pushed to the
back of her mind the memory of her mother's
ceaseless fretful demands.

'Independence?' he said slowly. 'Often that can
be just another word for being alone. I know because I've used it myself. But you don't have to
be alone, Carlotta. Here you have a place of
honour at my side. I have work to do here. You
could help.'

She wanted to cry out, 'Because a place of
honour at your side—without love—would be the
ultimate loneliness...worse than anything I could
endure without you.'

Instead she shook her head. 'I'd be hopeless.'
Her voice quivered. 'I—I don't even speak your
language.'

'You could learn—with Agenor's help, and
mine.'

'It will never work, believe me. You have to
let me go.' She took a deep breath. 'Now that we
can use the river again, I thought maybe you
could spare Pedrinho for a day to take me back
to Mariasanta.'

'Impossible.'

'No—no, it isn't. I swear I won't make any
trouble for you. We can put this whole miserable
mess behind us—and get on with our lives.'

'As if nothing had happened?' he questioned mockingly. '*Desculpe,* Carlotta. It is too late for that. Besides, the boat's engine is being repaired.'

'Oh.' Her shoulders slumped. 'But there must be some other way out of here, no matter what you say. You have to transport the rubber somehow, and——'

'You are grasping at straws, *querida*. And you seem to have forgotten something.' He paused. 'We have still to learn, after all, if there is to be a child.'

For a moment she was tempted to lie—to tell him she had positive proof that there wasn't going to be a baby, but somehow the words shrivelled on her lips. Instead she tried another gambit.

'But what about your family? They're obviously very important people. What will they say—when they find out you've married a total nobody?'

Riago shrugged a naked shoulder. 'No doubt my mother has already informed all my relations of my intentions. But their opinions no longer matter to me. As I've told you, I am estranged from my family.'

Charlie swallowed. 'Because—because of the girl you told me about?' she asked with difficulty. 'Your sister-in-law?'

'Because of her—yes.' His tone had hardened again, and his expression became suddenly remote. 'One day, perhaps, I will explain...'

'There's no need.' She already knew more about it than she wanted, she thought with pain. 'I laid my life at her feet'—oh, God... 'I—I understand.'

'I doubt that,' he said drily. 'But it's not important that you should. At least, not yet.' He lay back against the pillows. 'What matters is that you are to be my wife.'

'And that will make everything all right?'

'It is a beginning.' He surveyed her through half-closed eyes. 'You are wearing my gift, *carinha*, after all. And there is a saying, I think, that a diamond is forever.'

'So they say,' she admitted huskily.

'Then remember that well, and believe me, Carlotta, when I tell you I will never let you go.'

'Then there's no more to be said.' A little sigh trembled out of her, and she turned away. 'I—I'm sorry I woke you.'

As she reached the door she thought she heard him say her name, but she didn't pause, or look back.

She hardly slept that night. She lay staring into the darkness, trying to decide what to do. She listened as well—straining her ears—hoping and praying for the distant tell-tale rumble of thunder which would signal the approach of another storm, another cloudburst to flood the river and keep the visitors from Laragosa at bay for a few more precious hours and days.

But there was only silence, broken occasionally by the mournful howl of a monkey. The sound made her shiver, bringing home to her exactly what she might have to face if she tried to leave through the forest.

Yet there had to be routes in and out of the estate which the *caboclos*—the so-called 'men of the interior'—used to bring their raw latex to the processing plant. She would have to find a way to one of their settlements, and hope they would help her, she thought, her stomach churning uneasily.

Yet wasn't this what she'd wanted—some adventure in her humdrum existence? She just hadn't bargained for fate delivering the danger and excitement of a lifetime in the space of a few short days, that was all.

But I don't want any more, she told herself resolutely. I want to get out of here and get back to the monotony of my everyday life in Britain. That's what I need.

Once her normal routine had been reestablished she'd be able to forget everything that had happened here, she assured herself with a kind of desperation. One day she might even be able to remember Riago da Santana without feeling as if she was being wrenched apart, physically and emotionally. One day, perhaps...

The day dawned hot and sultry, with no sign of impending rain. If providence, in the shape of the weather, wasn't prepared to rescue her then she would have to take matters into her own hands, she realised grimly.

She began a dogged search through the *guarda-roupa*, pushing aside the flimsy dresses with impatient hands, and at last she found what she was looking for—a pair of tailored cream linen trousers, and a matching shirt. Not exactly jungle wear, she thought as she changed into them, but beggars couldn't be choosers.

Footwear was a problem. Fay Preston clearly had not been expected to step out of doors, but Charlie needed boots.

I'll have to borrow some, she thought grimly.

Riago's room was deserted, of course. Charlie had become accustomed to the fact that his working day began before sunrise. She trod cautiously over to the cupboard, deliberately ignoring the unmade bed and the memories it evoked, and extracted a pair of the high leather boots he wore, shaking them out first to make sure no unpleasant creature had decided to make its home in them. She had long, slender feet, but the boots were still too big, and she had to put on two pairs of his socks and pad the heels with paper before she could achieve a reasonable fit. She helped herself to a hat as well.

She took a long look at herself in the mirror, then gently unfastened the chain of the diamond pendant, and laid it down on the dressing chest. She would take nothing when she left but the few things she'd brought.

'I will never let you go.' The words sounded as clearly in her head as if he'd spoken them, as if he were there beside her, and for a moment she stared wildly round the room, seeking him. But she was alone.

Leaving the pendant for him to find was a symbolic act, she thought as she turned away. It severed the last link between them, telling him more clearly than any words could do that she had gone forever.

She'd intended to walk straight out of the room, but somehow she found herself at the side of the bed, her hand smoothing the indentation in the pillow where his head had rested.

My only love. Silently her lips formed the words. Goodbye.

CHAPTER EIGHT

PHILIP HUGHES was waiting in the hallway when Charlie emerged. He gave her a slow top-to-toe assessment as she stared stonily back, struggling to hang on to her composure.

'Planning an expedition?' he asked silkily.

'I think that's my business.'

'Don't be sore.' He fell into step beside her. 'The chances are neither of us is going to make it out of here alone. The sensible course is to join forces.'

She stared at him. 'But you didn't want to know...'

He shrugged. 'That was then. This is now. Things change.' He took her arm, pulling her into the *sala de estar* and closing the door behind them. 'So, what have you got planned?'

'Not a great deal,' she admitted reluctantly. 'I'd thought of commandeering the boat I arrived on, but it's out of action.'

'How convenient,' Philip said with something of a snap. 'Your arrogant *novio* thinks of everything. Coming within a hundred miles of the bastard was definitely a bad move.'

Charlie stiffened, jerking herself away from his grasp. 'He saved your life.'

'No, darling, he gave me a reprieve. I plan to save my own life by getting out of here, because this is not a healthy place to be.'

'Your amnesia,' she said, tight-lipped, 'seems to be improving fast. If it ever really existed.'

He shrugged, unabashed. 'A miracle cure, no less. So—no boat means going into the interior, which will suit me better anyway. I have to keep a rendezvous.'

'With whom?' Charlie's unease was increasing by the second.

'Let's just say some friends.'

'The same ones who hit you over the head and left you?' she demanded with irony.

'No.' For a moment his face looked ugly. Then, with a visible effort, he relaxed and gave her a smile. 'Let's agree not to ask each other too many questions, shall we, sweetheart? There's very little about me that you need to know.'

'I thought I knew quite a lot already,' Charlie said bitterly.

'Courtesy of Auntie Mary, I suppose.' His smile widened. 'Well, I always was her favourite. And it was nice of the old trout to leave me everything, even if I shan't be claiming my inheritance yet awhile.'

She looked at him in dismay. 'But the estate needs sorting out. Her solicitor is anxious to see you.'

'Tough,' Philip said succinctly. 'But I'm not throwing up the chance of the kind of fortune you only dream about for a bungalow in the sticks.'

'What fortune?'

He flicked her cheek with his finger. It was casually done, but it stung. 'There you go with those questions again,' he reproved. 'Do I ask you why you're running out on a member of the great and wealthy Santana clan?'

A dignified silence was the only response, she knew, but curiosity got the better of her.

'Why do you call them that?' she asked carefully.

'Because they're loaded, sweetheart, seriously so. One of the ancestors apparently foresaw the end of the rubber boom, and sank his money into other things as well. They have gold and bauxite mining holdings, as well as coffee and ranching interests in other parts of Brazil. So your auto-cratic Riago is a good catch—even if he has fallen temporarily on hard times.'

'I don't think what Riago is trying to do here can be classified as that,' Charlie said sharply.

'Ah, but there's obviously a lot he hasn't told you.' Philip's smile was almost limpid. 'You don't think he's here through his own choice, surely? No, sweetheart, this is a form of banishment, be-cause he offended against clan law. The story was the talk of the river a year or two back. I heard it myself in Manaus.' He paused. 'It seems there was this girl.'

'I know about her,' she cut in. 'She married his brother. End of story.'

'Is that what he says?' Philip shook his head. 'Well, actually, that's just half the story. Apparently the lordly Riago reacted badly to being passed over for another man. In fact, he got caught trying to force his attentions on the bride only a month or two after the wedding. His brother and he had a fight—a real knock-down affair—and Riago was kicked out of the palatial family home, and sent here to do penance.

'God knows if and when he'll ever be allowed back into the family fold,' he added with a shrug. 'But acquiring a wife of his own might be the first step on the long road back. I'm sure that explains a lot about his proprietorial attitude. You're an important part of his moral rehabilitation. Or did you think he'd fallen in love with you?'

'No.' Charlie winced inwardly at the jeering note in his voice. 'I—never thought that. But I'm not prepared to be…an aid to respectability either.'

'So what were you going to do? Just walk out of here? How far did you think you'd get?'

'I'm not that stupid,' she said shortly. 'But I haven't seen any vehicles since I've been here, apart from the jeep Riago drives himself, although there must be some that the estate workers use. After all, how did you get here?'

'I can't remember—and that's the truth,' he added wryly.

'Well, the obvious place to look is down at the processing plant,' she said slowly. 'But that's where Riago himself will be, and if we show up he'll suspect something. He's bound to.'

'That's not a problem,' Philip said. 'I happen to know that he's not at the processing plant today. He's engaged elsewhere.'

'How do you know that?' Charlie frowned.

'Just take my word for it.' He paused. 'Do you know how to get to the processing plant and how far it is?'

'Not exactly, but I've seen the route he takes in the jeep. Not that it really helps.'

Philip thought for a moment. 'Do the estate workers come to the house much?'

'Usually only when Riago's here,' she said. 'Or for medical treatment from Rosita.'

'What about the boy who interprets for you?'

'He comes nearly every day.'

'How does he get here?'

'I don't know,' Charlie confessed. 'It—it never occurred to me to ask.' She beat a clenched fist into the palm of her other hand. 'And I said I wasn't stupid.'

'Forget the recriminations,' he advised tersely. 'Are you expecting him today? Because, without him, we could be stranded here.'

Two hours passed slowly, and there was no sign of Agenor. As the time wore on Charlie's nerves became increasingly tattered. She was desperately conscious of the fact that Riago might return at any moment, so, while she strained her ears for the sound of an approaching engine, she dreaded it as well.

She had a number of unpleasant thoughts to mull over too, and uppermost in her mind was Philip's explanation of Riago's presence here on the Rio Tiajos. Gossip and hearsay it might be, but the story fitted the circumstances only too well, she told herself wretchedly.

Riago had admitted to her that his brother's wife had caused his estrangement from his family, but had been clearly reluctant to go into further details. The only reason for such reticence could be that he was ashamed.

Yes, he'd behaved badly, but loving this woman, then losing her to his brother, of all people, had created an explosive situation, especially if they'd all been living under one roof, as it seemed. Passion, mingled with anger and disappointment, must have got the better of him, she thought sadly.

But he'd paid a heavy price for his transgression. No one could deny that. And she could even understand, now, why he was so obsessed with family honour. The callous seduction of an innocent girl would have been yet another serious black mark on his record.

The fact that she'd run away from him wouldn't help his cause particularly either, she realised, but she couldn't afford to let herself think about that too deeply.

He was using her. That's what she had to remember. Using her because she... satisfied his requirements. And emotions, feelings, dreams, came nowhere because all of his belonged to someone else.

She tore her thoughts away from him with difficulty, and turned them instead to Philip Hughes, currently playing solitaire at a table by the window with a pack of cards he'd found in a cupboard.

He'd been as restless as a caged animal all morning, she thought irritably, either wandering in and out of the room, or prowling endlessly up and down it.

He seemed even more on edge than she was herself, and getting involved with him was probably the second most unwise thing she'd ever done in her life, she decided sombrely. He was trouble all the way down the line.

There was little doubt that he was up to his neck in something illegal, and she could only be thankful that his aunt would never know.

In fact, having him as a travelling companion for even part of the way was the last thing she wanted, she told herself flatly. But she seemed to be stuck with him, at least until they were clear of the *fazenda*, when they could go their separate ways.

It was a depressing and uncomfortable thought, but Charlie had to admit she'd have had difficulty in calling anything remotely cheerful to mind at the moment.

She was debating whether or not to ring for yet another tray of coffee when Agenor walked in.

'*Senhorita.*' He stared at her, concerned. 'Is wrong, something?'

She realised she'd been gaping at him, open-mouthed, as if he were some apparition, and rallied hastily, aware that Philip was getting to his feet.

'Have you only just arrived, Agenor? How did you get here?'

'In the truck of my cousin, as always, *senhorita*. If I am late I regret, but——'

'It doesn't matter,' Philip cut brusquely across the careful apology. 'Is your cousin still around?'

'*Sim, senhor.* He speaks with Rosita.'

'That's good,' Philip said. 'Then we can have a word with him too.'

He took Charlie's arm and hustled her towards the door.

'I need to fetch my bag,' she hissed at him urgently.

'To hell with it.' His grip didn't relax one iota. 'The truck is more important than your bits and pieces.'

There was a fenced-off area behind the kitchens where hens pecked at the ground and a couple of pigs were rooting busily. The truck was parked just beyond this. It was empty, and the keys were in the ignition.

'Our first piece of luck,' Philip muttered, then looked at her with sudden misgiving. 'I hope you can drive the bloody thing.'

'Yes,' she said shortly.

Rather to her surprise, the truck started at her first, tentative effort. As they moved away Charlie saw in the mirror that Pedrinho had suddenly appeared in the rear doorway with Rosita at his side.

If she hadn't been so tense and miserable the expression of dumbfounded horror on their faces would have been almost amusing. Pedrinho even threw down his hat and jumped on it.

'Take the track to the processing plant,' Philip ordered. 'I'll get my bearings from there.'

'We should have brought a map.' The truck screeched as Charlie fumbled a gear.

'I did.' He produced one from inside his shirt. 'I'm sure Senhor da Santana can spare it. He seemed to have about a dozen of them in his office.'

'You shouldn't have gone in there,' Charlie protested. 'It's private.'

He laughed derisively. 'Tell me about it. You surely didn't think I was going to leave him that radio to track us with?'

'You've destroyed his radio?' Her voice cracked in dismay. 'But the estate relies on it. Supposing there's an emergency?'

'My emergency comes first,' he said harshly. 'Do you think I give a damn what happens to a handful of rubber-grubbing peasants and their high and mighty master? We're not playing games, sweetheart.'

'Don't call me that,' she snapped, struggling with the wheel as the truck lurched drunkenly over a deep rut in the track.

'What name do you want, then—Carlotta?' he gibed, and she flushed deeply.

'No,' she said in a stifled voice.

Philip laughed. 'If I didn't know better, *senhorita*, I'd say you could be in love with the black sheep of the Santana family.'

'Oh, leave me alone,' she flung at him. 'You don't want my questions. Well, I can do without your speculation.'

He shrugged. 'Suit yourself,' he said and lapsed into silence.

They seemed to be vanishing down the centre of some vast green tunnel, Charlie thought as she struggled with the truck, which had a mind of its own. She had the curious sensation that, if she looked back over her shoulder, she would find the forest had closed in behind them, absorbing them into its world of tall trunks, leafy canopies and writhing creepers, so that they would never be found again.

Oh, stop it, she adjured herself. Riago and everyone else uses this track each day with perfect safety. You're just letting your imagination run away with you.

She felt even more foolish when a sudden gleam of water through the trees told her that the track, which seemed to lead inland, in fact ran parallel with the Rio Tiajos, or one of its tributaries, as she'd hoped. As long as she followed the river she couldn't get lost.

But, all the same, it was with real relief that she saw a thin trail of smoke rising above the trees, and realised they were coming to houses.

The actual settlement where the estate workers lived was bigger than she'd expected. The thatched cabins varied in size and were built in clusters. Women stood in the doorways with children playing at their feet. When they saw the truck, with Charlie at the wheel, they began pointing and shouting with excitement.

'Keep going,' Philip said tersely. 'Don't slow down.'

'I suppose you'd like me to drive straight over them,' she returned through gritted teeth. 'I didn't realise we'd attract so much attention. Now they'll be able to tell Riago exactly which direction we took.'

Philip gave another shrug. 'By that time we'll be long gone,' he said flatly.

She glanced at him in amazement. 'You think the *caboclos* won't be able to track us?'

'Not any further than the landing strip, unless they've got wings,' he retorted.

'You mean you're getting a plane out of here?' Charlie gasped. 'But that's impossible. Nothing could land or take off.'

He smiled sourly. 'It's almost a scheduled flight,' he countered. 'The same bush aircraft has been delivering and collecting me for quite some time.'

'To prospect for gold?'

'I tried that for a while up near Itaituba, but it was too much like hard work. Now I act as a kind of middleman.'

They were almost out of the settlement by now. Away on the left Charlie could see a buzz of activity round several large corrugated-iron buildings, which, she guessed must be the processing plant. There was a heavy chemical smell in the humid air, and she closed her throat against it, wiping a bead of sweat from her eyes.

She said, 'You're mixed up with the *garimpeiros*, aren't you, the illegal prospectors? Riago told me—warned me about them.'

He laughed. 'I'm sure he did. But underneath they're just simple men trying to make their fortunes. I buy the stones from them *brute*—that's uncut to you—and take them to my principals in Manaus.' He was silent for a moment. When he spoke again his voice was soft, like a lover's. 'You've no idea the hold that gemstones can get on you. I've handled amethysts the size of your hand...topazes like oranges, or as smoky as mist—and diamonds, beautiful clearwater diamonds. They're the best of all, like exquisite glittering mirrors into a man's soul.'

'Very poetic,' Charlie said scornfully. 'However, I presume these same simple men are the ones who injured you and left you sick with malaria.'

'A small matter of some commission,' he said. 'These things happen, even in the best circles. But it does mean, unfortunately, that my career locally has come to an end. I'm getting out for good—going up to Bolivia. That's what I love about South America. So many countries. So many opportunities for the—er—entrepreneur.'

'Is that how you see yourself?' Charlie asked with irony. 'I thought "smuggler" was the more usual term.'

'You've got a sharp little tongue, darling,' he said gently. 'I advise you to be careful how you use it. The people I work with tend to be low on humour.'

She was just about to tell him she didn't give a damn about the people he worked with, or any part of any criminal organisation, when a man suddenly appeared on the track in front of her, frantically waving his arms.

'Don't stop.' Philip's voice was like the lash of a whip.

Charlie sent him a look of loathing, and braked hard. She'd recognised the man at once. It was Manoel, the plantation foreman. He almost tore the truck door open, staring up at her in bewilderment and appeal, before embarking on a flood of excited Portuguese.

'*Não percebo,*' Charlie broke in when he paused for breath. 'I'm sorry, I don't understand.'

'He says his wife's having her baby,' Philip translated curtly. 'Tell him you'll send him a cigar, and get this bloody truck moving.'

'But that's Ana Maria!' Charlie exclaimed, distressed. 'Oh, God, that must be why Pedrinho came to the house this morning—to get Rosita...because of the baby.'

'These people breed like flies. What's all the fuss about?'

His callousness appalled her. 'Her other babies have died. That's why she needs Rosita. She's a good midwife. If we hadn't taken the truck she'd be here now, looking after Ana Maria. And we've prevented it.'

'You're breaking my heart. Now shift.'

Cold fury hardened her sudden resolution. 'I'll do nothing of the sort,' she said. 'There's a child's life at stake here. Manoel's a good man— one of Riago's most trusted workers. He deserves the best care for his wife that we can give. I'm going back to the *fazenda* to get Rosita.'

'Oh, no, you're not,' he said savagely. 'I thought you might be trouble, so I decided to take a hostage. Perhaps this will persuade you to continue with the journey.' He reached into the pocket of his shirt and took out the diamond pendant, dangling it tauntingly in front of her. The sun caught the facets of the stone, turning them to a blaze of fire.

Her throat tightened in anguish. 'Where did you get that?'

'I saw you weren't wearing it this morning, so I had a look round.' He was openly triumphant. 'Call it your plane fare out of here.'

'I'm not catching any plane,' she said thickly. 'I wouldn't travel one more yard with you.'

'Then you're a fool. You want out. I'm prepared to take you along.' His voice grated. 'But I'm not jeopardising everything for the sake of some brat. I've got a cache of *brute* diamonds—the commission I was telling you about—hidden in a safe place, in addition to this little beauty. We're going to collect them, and then we're going to catch that plane before that bastard Santana brings the military down on the lot of us. I heard him on the radio arranging it first thing today. Well, I'm not interested in spending the next years of my life in a Brazilian gaol. So drive this truck and get us out of here.'

Charlie shook her head. 'No way,' she said. 'You're on your own. And I'm thankful your aunt will never know what you've become.'

Philip shrugged. 'Save me the sickly sentiment,' he said harshly. 'Stay and play *dona da casa* if that's what you want. But I'm keeping the Santana diamond. I reckon you owe it to me—compensation for the money you wheedled out of Auntie Mary, you bitch.'

He lunged across at her, impelling Charlie towards the open door of the truck, then hit her full across the face with his open hand. The pain almost stunned her, and she tasted blood on her mouth as she lost her balance and fell backwards.

Hands seized her, and dragged her clear of the cabin. Manoel's voice, oddly fuzzy, cried out, *'Senhorita. Meu Deus, Senhorita Carlotta.'*

She found she was lying on the path. The truck, with Philip at the wheel, was lurching away, the engine screaming, and Manoel was running after it, waving his fists and shouting.

She yelled, *'Venha cá, Manoel*—come back,' with all her might.

He obeyed with open reluctance.

'Let him go,' she said, forcing the words from her sore and swollen mouth as Manoel helped her to her feet. 'Just let him go.'

Manoel was clearly torn between his concern for her and his worry for Ana Maria.

'Rosita?' he asked, staring round him as if expecting her to materialise suddenly from the bushes.

'Desculpe, Manoel,' she said gently. 'She isn't here. She's still at the house.'

Manoel looked as if he was about to burst into tears. He broke into another agitated gabble of words, and Charlie put a detaining hand on his arm.

'We will send someone,' she said haltingly in his own language. *'Onde é Ana Maria?'*

Manoel had one of the largest houses in the settlement. It was sparsely furnished, but spotlessly clean. Ana Maria was on the bed in the inner room, twisting from side to side, and moaning under her breath. An elderly woman sat in a corner of the room, jabbering something which sounded like incantations, and two younger girls stood by the bed in self-conscious helplessness.

They all gaped at Charlie as she came in. She tried to smile reassuringly down at the pregnant girl, but her mouth hurt too much. Manoel had commandeered an elderly jeep and was on his way to the *fazenda*, although Charlie was sure that Rosita and Pedrinho would have set off on foot by now.

She tried to tell Ana Maria that help was coming, but the girl just stared up at her, her eyes glazed with pain and incomprehension, so she said, *'Calma,'* several times instead.

And, oddly enough, her presence did seem to be having a tranquillising effect. Ana Maria stopped throwing herself about, and took hold of Charlie's hand, clinging to it as if it was a lifeline.

In films they always tell people to boil water, she thought. She tried saying *'agua'*, and the old woman grunted and shuffled out, coming back almost at once with a dipper of cold water.

Well, it was better than nothing, Charlie thought, dampening her own clean handkerchief and gently wiping Ana Maria's mouth and forehead with it. The girl was obviously terrified, her swollen body wet with perspiration, and her breathing shallow.

So many previous disappointments, Charlie thought wretchedly. And if she loses this baby as well it will be partly my fault.

She bent towards her, gently squeezing her fingers. 'It's going to be all right, Ana Maria,' she whispered. 'You're going to have a son—a

big, healthy boy who'll probably play football
for Brazil. It's going to be all right.'

She went on talking quietly, keeping her voice
level, almost hypnotic, as the minutes dragged
past. The room was getting like a sauna, and she
could feel beads of sweat trickling down her nose,
and running between her breasts and shoulder-
blades. The other women had retired to the
doorway, and stood watching, so she and Ana
Maria were virtually alone.

She talked about her life in England, the impulse that had brought her here, and the unre-
solved conflict which had forced her to remain.

'And now, just when I have the chance to leave,
I blow it—because I feel responsible. Because I
suddenly seem to care about what goes on here
on the plantation. And I can't afford to care. I
could have gone, and I should have done. So why
am I still here? Tell me that.'

Ana Maria moaned, then cried out, her body
twisting awkwardly. Charlie swallowed nervously, stroking her forehead, smoothing back
the damp hair. 'It's OK,' she soothed. 'Rosita
will be here soon. She only has to come from the
house. She can't take much longer.'

Ana Maria, of course, didn't understand a
word she was saying, so just who was she trying
to convince? she asked herself.

Meanwhile, even her untrained eyes could see
that a new phase in the girl's labour was beginning. She tried desperately to remember all the
things that her sister Sonia had told her self-
importantly about Christopher being born. She
wished now she'd paid more attention to Sonia's

complacent stories about being the star of her natural childbirth classes in the first instance, and subsequently about her stoical endurance during the actual heroic struggle to bring Christopher into the world.

But that had been with all the resources a private nursing home could provide. Sonia's experiences would hardly correlate with Ana Maria's in this two-roomed house in the rain forest. No gas and air here, or sterile conditions, and no incubator for a baby in trouble.

Ana Maria's hand convulsively tightened its grip on hers. She was grunting, trying to sit up, her eyes glassy with a new and powerful concentration, the veins standing out on her forehead.

Oh, God, Charlie thought despairingly. The baby's coming. It's coming now. What can I do?

She turned, gesturing frantically at the old woman, who began to rock backwards and forwards, making strange wailing noises.

'A lot of help you are,' Charlie snapped, her nerves fraying. *'Venha cá,'* she commanded the women in the doorway, but they backed away, hands pressed to their mouths.

Ana Maria gave a kind of feral roar, halfway between a scream of agony and a shout of triumph. Charlie moved frantically to the end of the bed, just in time to receive the baby—crimson, slippery and a boy—in her shaking hands. For a moment the child lay, his limbs moving almost questingly, as if missing the warmth and security of the womb, then his mouth opened and a cry of wavering outrage filled the room.

Through a blur of swift tears Charlie wiped his nose and mouth clean, and put him in Ana Maria's arms.

There was a sudden hubbub in the outer room, and Rosita flew in, with Manoel behind her, checking as she saw the girl on the bed, her pale, weary face alight with joy as she offered her son her breast. Then she took in Charlie's presence, and a squawk of dismay escaped her. Exclamations and commands began issuing from her like a rattle of machine-gun fire, and Charlie found herself being hustled out of the way as the older woman took charge.

She went without protest, feeling totally limp. She was thankful she wasn't being called on to cut the umbilical cord, or perform any further service, because she wasn't sure she could cope. As it was, the events of the past half-hour were certainly some of the most telling in her life so far, and she was grateful for having shared them.

Agenor came to her side. '*Senhorita*—you are here.' His face was bewildered. 'The *patrão*—he think you gone. He follow—go search with many soldiers.'

She said gently, 'It's all right, Agenor. I'm quite safe, as you see.'

In a little while Manoel came to her. Beaming with pride, he took her hand and kissed it, and burst into impassioned speech.

'He wishes to thank you, *senhorita*, for the safety of his son,' Agenor translated. 'Also Ana Maria, if you will go to her.'

'But I didn't do anything,' Charlie protested. 'I was just—here.'

She was ushered back into the inner room. Ana Maria was cradling the baby in her arms, her face worshipful.

'*Obrigada, senhorita,*' she whispered, holding up the small bundle.

Charlie stared down at the baby's angry, puckered face. She put out a finger, and felt the tiny hand grasp it firmly. And in that moment she knew, instinctively and unquestionably, that she was indeed carrying Riago's child inside her. Her throat tightened uncontrollably.

What can I do? she thought. Oh, God, what can I do?

CHAPTER NINE

CHARLIE was very quiet during the jeep ride back to the house. Her companions were subdued as well, their elation over the safe birth of Manoel's son clearly tempered by concern for Riago.

Although she'd redeemed herself to some extent by acting as emergency midwife to Ana Maria, Charlie was conscious that she was in disgrace for helping Philip Hughes—'that worthless one', as Agenor, his dark eyes openly censorious, had called him—to escape, and therefore exposing the *patrão* to the risks of hunting him down in the rain forest.

Without her intervention Philip, she was given to understand, would simply have been detained at the *fazenda* without danger to anyone. And if she had not been seen to accompany him Riago would have had no reason to take an active role in the search for him.

Now there were fears, Agenor told her, that he might be caught in the crossfire in the vicious little war which had been raging for months between the *garimpeiros* and the wealthy gem dealers in Manaus. A war in which Philip Hughes had been wounded, several others had died, and which the military authorities were determined to end, along with the wholesale smuggling of uncut stones.

To save himself the *inglês* would have spoken, Agenor said grimly. He would have taken the soldiers to the hidden landing strips in the jungle, and to the secret camps of the *garimpeiros*. Now he was free to warn his *compadres* on both sides, so the centre of their operations would be changed, the war would drag on, and more would be killed.

'But I couldn't stop him stealing the truck,' Charlie protested in her own defence.

'Pedrinho could stop.' Agenor's face was reproachful. 'But because you in truck, *senhorita*, he could not use gun.'

And there was no real answer to that, Charlie thought wearily.

The house was silent too, and seemed strangely deserted. The maids weren't singing about their work today, and there was none of the distant babble of laughter and talk from the kitchen that she'd become accustomed to.

It's as if there's been a death, she thought, cold panic gripping her. But there hasn't been, and I'm not even going to let myself consider it as a possibility.

But she couldn't rid herself of the sense of guilt which was oppressing her as she wandered from one room to another. She'd allowed herself to ignore Philip's questionable behaviour, overlook the obvious flaws in his character, oblivious to everything but her need to escape from Riago and this loveless marriage he was seeking to impose on her.

But that no longer seemed to matter—not now she had to face the possibility that she could be his widow before she'd ever been his wife.

She walked into Riago's room, and stood staring across at the bed. It had been made during her absence, and the carefully smoothed cover and pristine linen emitted a kind of chill.

She walked across and sat down on the bed, pressing a protective hand to her abdomen. Ana Maria had touched her in the same way only a little while ago, she remembered with a pang. Some of the onlookers who'd crowded into the room had been clearly scandalised by her familiarity with the *patrão's* bride, but Charlie knew that the other girl, made percipient perhaps by the joy of her own motherhood, had read her secret in her face, and was silently sharing the knowledge of it with her.

It was wrong—all of it. Out of the casual passion of a night a child would come who might never know his father.

It had been a farce from the beginning, she told herself. A comedy of errors which had turned suddenly to melodrama, and now seemed to be plunging towards tragedy.

She had thought that she'd already paid, with her body, the only ransom that would be demanded of her. But Riago had gone after her, believing her to be Philip's hostage, and this time he might be the one to pay an even darker ransom—in blood.

She shuddered, hugging herself almost convulsively, as if that would dam back the fear and the wretchedness.

'Send him back to me,' she whispered. 'Please send him back safely, and I'll be his on whatever terms he chooses.'

She curled up on the bed, pressing her face into the pillow, seeking some reminder of him—some lingering trace of the scent of his skin, a breath of the cologne he sometimes used. But there was nothing. No comfort for her.

She remained where she was, huddled up, like a small animal seeking sanctuary, and, as the minutes turned into hours, at last she fell asleep.

There were dreams in that sleep. Dreams of the green tunnel in the forest, where dark-faced men waited with guns on their hips and machetes in their hands. At the end of the tunnel she seemed to see Riago, but when she tried to call his name and go to him Philip Hughes appeared beside him, stepping between them, barring her way, taunting her with the diamond pendant which dangled from his fingers.

She saw them struggling together, the two figures receding and becoming smaller, as if she were looking down the wrong end of a telescope, so that when one fell she could not see which it was. She began to run, her feet tangling in creepers and ferns, the branches of unnamed trees slashing at her as she tried to push past them. And as she ran the tiny tableau of the fallen man and his conqueror became ever-smaller, and she knew she had to reach them before it disappeared completely. The breath was labouring in her lungs, and when she tried to scream no sound emerged.

She came awake very suddenly, her body
soaked with sweat. She sat up, still trembling
from reaction, and saw, in the fading daylight,
Riago watching her from the doorway.

He was leaning heavily against one of the posts,
deeply dishevelled, a jacket draped awkwardly
over one shoulder, his face haggard with
weariness and strain.

For an endless moment they looked at each
other in taut silence.

Then he said very quietly, 'Why did you come
back?'

Slowly Charlie pushed her hair back from her
face. She said, 'I—I never really went away.
Didn't they tell you? I got to the settlement, and
Ana Maria was having her baby—so I stayed.'
She added, swiftly and rather ridiculously,
'They're going to call it Carlos—after me.'

He moved a hand dismissively, grimacing as if
he was in pain. 'You left—you went with him,
the *inglês*.' That worthless one. Agenor's contemptuous phrase seemed to hang in the air between them. Riago went on, 'He stole the truck
and took you with him.'

'That was the intention, yes.' She folded her
arms across her breasts, feeling suddenly cold.

'What was his name? You knew it, didn't you,
Carlotta? You knew him.' His eyes never left her
face.

'Yes—in a way.' She swallowed. 'His name is
Philip Hughes.' The fact that Riago had used the
past tense had not been lost on her. 'Tell me—
is he—is he . . . ?'

'He is dead, yes. Shot.'

She ran her tongue over her dry lips. 'Did you kill him?'

He shook his head slowly. 'No, he was killed running towards a plane. Someone on the aircraft killed him with a burst of machine-gun fire. It seems, like the *garimpeiros*, they had no further use for him.'

'I see.' She remembered the photograph of the smiling young man, and his aunt's wistful pride, and tears tightened her throat.

His voice was gentle, but it seemed to come from a great distance. 'You told me once you had come here to find someone. Was it this man—this *inglês*?'

'Yes, but you don't understand——'

'What is there to understand?' Riago shrugged, his face twisting momentarily.

'A great deal.' And how idiotic it all sounded in retrospect, she thought bitterly. The Philip Hughes she'd hoped to find had been an illusion—a figment of her imagination. How could she explain that to the hard sceptical face of the man watching her from the doorway? She made an effort. 'You see—I never really knew him at all.'

'And yet, although he was clearly a liar and almost certainly a criminal, you cared enough about him to try and help him to escape. You cared enough to trust him with your life—and more?' How cold he sounded. How remote.

'No. He was supposed to be helping me.' Her own voice was weary with self-derision. 'Only it all went wrong. I should have seen he was dangerous—not to be trusted—only, I suppose,

I wanted to...preserve the illusion a little bit longer.'

'Ah.' He smiled faintly. 'Illusions. Now those, *querida*, I can understand. I have suffered from them myself, after all. But no longer.' He paused, then said flatly, 'Tomorrow, when the boat comes from Laragosa, I will send you back to the mission with Padre Gaspar. He will see that you get safely to Manaus, or wherever you wish to go.'

'You're sending me away?' Her voice cracked a little. 'But why?'

'Because, as you have said so often, I have no right to keep you here.' His tone hardened. 'And, as you were prepared to leave with another man, I do not think that even my household and family would now consider I had any further obligation towards you.'

'But it wasn't like that.' Charlie scrambled up on to her knees. 'Riago—please listen...'

He shook his head. 'No, I've heard enough. This is indeed today's world with all its greed and violence, so it is foolish to try and live according to the traditions of the past. To try—as you say—to preserve the illusion. So—you are set free.'

She said unevenly, 'Riago—please don't do this...'

'Is something wrong?' The tired voice bit. 'Are you afraid that I will expect you to leave empty-handed? No, *carinha*, you need not fear.' He held out his hand. 'This should cover the cost of your expenses and any...inconvenience you might have suffered.'

She climbed slowly and stiffly down from the bed, and walked towards him, searching desperately in his face for the smile in his eyes, the softening of the firm mouth, which, almost unconsciously, she'd come to expect when he saw her. But there was nothing.

She said, 'I don't want anything, Riago—except for you to listen to me and believe me.'

'But you must take this. It is yours, after all. The gift I made to you.' The outstretched hand unclenched, as if with an effort, and Charlie saw the diamond glittering coldly in his palm. 'Captain Martinho found it on the *inglês*,' he continued almost conversationally. 'I suggest that if you give it away again, Carlotta, you find a worthier object for your generosity.'

The last word was uttered with a kind of gasp, and as Charlie watched, her lips parting in horror, Riago's knees began to buckle, and he slid, almost in slow motion, down the door-post to the floor, and lay there. The jacket slipped from his shoulder, and she saw with shocked incredulity the dark red stain of blood spreading across his shirt.

She began to shake her head from side to side in a kind of wild negation, whispering his name as she did so.

It was only when Rosita, Pedrinho and the others arrived, crowding into the doorway, that she realised she was screaming.

'Is bullet in shoulder, *senhorita*. We must take out.'

Charlie, huddled on one of the sofas in the *sala de estar*, stared up at Agenor. They had given her coffee laced with *cachaça*—the fiery local white rum—to drink, but it hadn't stopped her trembling, or warmed the icy chill inside her. Perhaps nothing would ever again.

She'd watched them lifting Riago's limp body on to the bed, seen the grey tinge underlying the bronze of his skin, and that dreadful stain— growing, spreading . . .

And he'd said nothing, she thought wonder-ingly. No one had known he'd been wounded.

She swallowed down the fear and nausea and tried to speak calmly. 'How can we? We're not doctors.'

Agenor shrugged. 'Pedrinho has take out bullet before—one, two times, maybe. Rosita say bullet go bad in body—make fever.'

She could believe it in this environment, in this climate, where infections, even from the smallest graze, could run rife without treatment.

'We hurry, *senhorita*,' Agenor pressed her. 'Senhor Don Riago lose much blood.'

She said huskily, 'Then—I suppose we'd better try.'

Riago's face looked shadowed against the snowy pillows. He was muttering faintly, his body moving feebly and restlessly under the covers. Charlie went over to the bed, and looked down at him, her throat tightening.

Beside her, Agenor spoke in a low voice. 'It is bad, *senhorita*. He say no to Pedrinho, also to Rosita, who has nursed him since baby. All his life he fight—but no more.'

'We'll see about that,' Charlie said fiercely. 'Send everyone out except Rosita and Pedrinho.'

While her instructions were being obeyed she sat down on the bed, capturing Riago's hand in both hers.

She bent forward until her lips were almost grazing his ear, her voice low and hurried. 'You're going to fight—do you hear me? You're not going to give up. Too much depends on you for that, and too many people. You say you want to send me away—well, you can tell me that when you're well and strong again. Because, until then, I'm staying—and I'm making the decisions.'

The dark eyes opened and stared at her without recognition.

'*Não,*' his voice croaked. '*Não. Basta. Podo ir.*'

'No one's going anywhere,' Charlie said firmly. She could see Rosita on the other side of the bed, busying herself with a basin and dressings. Pedrinho was standing beside her, and as Charlie nodded he stepped forward. She caught a glimpse of the gleam of steel in Pedrinho's stubby fingers, and suppressed a shudder.

Riago half reared up in the bed, away from Pedrinho, then sank back with a groan. '*Não,*' he repeated hoarsely.

'*Senhorita.*' Agenor had reappeared at her side. '*Patrão* no move. You must hold still for Pedrinho.'

How can I do that? Charlie asked herself in dismay.

Weak as he was, Riago was probably stronger than her anyway. And, if she used all the force she was capable of, she might hurt him.

They were all watching her, she realised, Pedrinho's brown face wrinkled with anxiety as he waited.

She clearly had to do something, but what?

Riago's lips parted on a sigh of pain, and, obeying her instinct, Charlie lifted herself on to the bed and lay beside him.

She said quietly, '*Calma, namorado,*' then, cradling his head in her hands, put her mouth firmly and deliberately on his. It was the first time in her life she'd ever kissed a man or taken any kind of sexual initiative, she realised as she let her tongue trail sweetly and seductively along the line of his lower lip.

For a moment Riago was quiescent. He might not be responding, she thought, but at least he wasn't pushing her away. She bent closer to him, pressing her breasts against his uninjured arm.

She was aware of Pedrinho stepping forward, and closed her eyes, deepening the kiss, murmuring soft sounds of endearment against Riago's mouth.

'It's all right, darling,' she whispered frantically as she felt his body arch up in pain and shock. 'Everything's going to be all right.' That was the second such promise she'd made in the past twenty-four hours, she realised ironically. And both times she'd been promising life. For Ana Maria it had all come right. Please God, let it be no less for Riago. Let it be true, she thought desperately.

She smoothed the sweat-dampened hair. 'It will all be fine. But you've got to keep still. Keep still for me.'

She could hear the rasp of Pedrinho's breathing as he worked, and Rosita's voice, tear-choked, as she muttered an endless stream of words, which might have been prayers.

She held Riago tightly, locking her mouth to his, smothering the involuntary groans which rose in his throat, trying to breathe some of her own vitality into his lungs.

'It will soon be over,' she told him. Dear God, let it soon be over. Soon . . .

She heard Pedrinho make a low triumphant sound, and Riago's body went suddenly limp in her arms.

She lifted her head slowly and stared at them all through tear-glazed eyes.

'You've killed him,' she said dully. 'He's dead.'

'*Não, senhorita.*' Agenor was horrified. 'Bullet out. Is faint only.'

She felt like fainting herself, particularly when Pedrinho tried, proudly, to show her the bullet lying in its basin. Rosita had stopped praying, and had moved into action, staunching the blood and deftly cleaning and dressing the wound. Her shrewd dark eyes looked across the bed at Charlie, taking in the girl's pale face and quivering mouth.

'You come away now, *senhorita*,' Agenor urged. 'Rosita say you do enough. You rest.'

'I want to stay with the *senhor.*'

'Rosita say the *senhor* rest too. She give special drink with herbs—make sleep. For you, also.'

Agenor took her arm firmly but respectfully, helping her to get up.

For a moment she wanted to resist, but she knew it would do no good. A solitary vigil beside his bed would benefit no one. It would be far better for Riago to find her with him—when he recovered consciousness.

She'd almost thought 'if', she realised with a pang. But she wasn't going to think like that. She wouldn't consider any alternative but his restoration to full health and vigour.

Whether he still wanted her or not would, of course, be another matter. But she couldn't think about that, either. Not now...

Somehow she found herself back in her own room, but she couldn't relax. Couldn't stop her mind plodding in weary circles. She sat on the bed, gripping the edge with both hands, staring into space, trying to keep her thoughts, her fears at bay.

Riago's stormy, devastating arrival in her life had only been a comparatively short time ago, she remembered wonderingly. Yet since that first meeting she seemed to have encompassed a whole lifetime of experience and emotion. Of pleasure and pain. Of jealousy and anguished longing. To lose him now would create some black and bottomless void in which she would be lost eternally.

Fate had brought her here to find him. She knew that now. And surely that same fate wouldn't be so cruel as to take him from her, now that she knew—and was prepared to admit—exactly what he meant to her.

He may never know I love him, she thought. And on the wings of that came the equally chilling realisation—When I tell him, will he care? Will it make even the smallest difference?

She bowed her head, feeling tears burning in her throat. Then the door opened and Rosita surged in.

It was rather, Charlie thought later, like being caught up in a large and comforting whirlwind, if there could be such a thing. She found herself being firmly divested of her clothes, and tucked into bed, as if she were a child. Then, with Rosita's arm around her shoulders, she was made to sip the promised herb drink, which was not as unpalatable as its murky green colour suggested. And after that everything slipped into a confused but pleasant haze.

It was broad daylight when she awoke, startled into consciousness by Rosita's hand shaking her excitedly.

She sat up instantly. 'What is it? The *senhor*?'

'*Sim.*' Rosita nodded vigorously, the worried expression on her face filling Charlie with sick panic.

'Oh, God.' Charlie scrambled out of bed, reaching instinctively for the amethyst robe. 'What's happened? Is he worse?'

Rosita shrugged in incomprehension, then snatched the robe away, indicating with a nod that Charlie should put on the day clothes already laid out for her instead.

'Are you crazy?' Charlie tried to grab the robe back. 'If it's an...an emergency anything will do.'

But Rosita's expression was mulish, her gesture towards the waiting pile of clothes adamant.

'Oh, for heaven's sake,' Charlie said, exasperated, as she began to throw on her clothes. But it didn't finish there. Rosita gave her a hawk-eyed inspection, then handed her a hairbrush.

I don't believe this, Charlie thought as she gave her hair a few perfunctory strokes. Riago could be terribly sick. He could even be dying—and she's fussing about messy hair and too many buttons unfastened on my shirt. What does it matter—what does anything matter?

But, as she left her room and turned towards his, Rosita blocked her once more, her face firm, indicating that Charlie should follow her in the opposite direction.

'But I want to go to the *senhor*,' Charlie protested, finding herself being ruthlessly and inexorably propelled instead towards the *sala de estar*.

'Senhor da Santana, *sim*,' Rosita nodded, and Charlie's bewilderment grew. She tried to hang back.

'Are you telling me he's in the sitting-room? That you've allowed him to get up already?' she demanded, anger and outrage making her forget the language barrier. 'What's the matter with you all? Are you trying to kill him?'

Yet maybe Riago had insisted on getting up, it occurred to her with chilling force. Perhaps, however weak he still felt, he had something to say to her that he wanted to be on his feet for. And that could mean only one thing . . .

He was going to tell her to go, she thought, her stomach churning in sudden nausea.

Rosita, still gripping her arm, burst into a stream of excited chatter, then, throwing open the door of the *sala*, almost pushed Charlie into the room.

Two men confronted her, both strangers. For a moment she was icily still, wondering if they were police of some kind, come to arrest her for helping Philip Hughes. Then she saw they were smiling, albeit awkwardly.

She lifted her chin. *'Quem é o senhor?'* she demanded, looking at the taller of the two. *'Que quer?'*

The man she was addressing stepped forward. He was more formally dressed than she was accustomed to seeing, and his hair was greying not unattractively at the temples. She thought, He reminds me of someone . . .

'Senhorita Graham?' He made her a slight bow. His voice was deep and heavily accented. 'This is an honour for me. Permit me to present myself. I am Jorge da Santana.'

Her lips parted in astonishment. No wonder he'd seemed vaguely familiar. Now that she looked at him properly she could see the resemblance. But what was he, of all people in the world, doing here?

'How do you do?' She shook hands politely, glancing enquiringly at the other man, who was plainly older, his hair grizzled, his face weatherbeaten and shrewd.

'*Desculpe*. This is Padre Gaspar, whom you were expecting, I think.'

Charlie gasped. In all the uproar she'd forgotten about the boat bringing the priest from Laragosa. And not just the priest.

'Wasn't there supposed to be a doctor too?' she asked urgently.

'Dr Afonza is even now with my brother,' Jorge da Santana informed her gravely.

'That's wonderful,' she said with real relief. She ran her tongue round her lips. 'You know, of course—they'll have told you what happened—how Riago came to be shot?' She turned to the priest. 'I—I'm afraid you've had a wasted journey, Padre.'

The thin lips softened into a smile of surprising sweetness. '*De nada, senhorita*. I am sorry if the wedding is not to take place, of course, but glad that I am not required for any other reason.'

Charlie looked down at the floor. 'We don't know that,' she said in a low voice. 'Not yet. Pedrinho had to get the bullet out. There was so much blood...'

Jorge da Santana made a stifled sound. 'My brother,' he said. 'I blame myself. But for me, he would not be here. This terrible thing could not have happened. I only hope he will forgive me.'

The priest gave him a dry look. 'A man of Riago's strength does not succumb to a bullet in the shoulder, *amigo*. He will be spared for you to put an end to this quarrel. I guarantee it.'

Jorge da Santana groaned. 'Thank God.'

'As we all should, at each hour of each day,' Padre Gaspar said with kindly finality. 'Dr Afonza should have finished his examination by now. Perhaps we can visit the patient, with your permission, *senhorita*.'

'Of course,' Charlie said awkwardly. 'Please come with me.'

Rosita admitted them to the bedroom, where the doctor, a burly man with a beard, was washing his hands. Her face was solemn, but she gave Charlie a reassuring smile and a pat.

'How is he?' Jorge da Santana asked softly.

'He needs rest, nourishment and the antibiotics I have given him,' came the reply in English, as Dr Afonza dried his hands on a towel, inclining his head politely to Charlie as he did so. 'But, above all, rest, so I have administered a mild sedative.'

'May I speak with him? There is so much that I must say.'

Dr Afonza frowned. 'And plenty of time ahead to say it in,' he said with a faintly quelling look. 'For now, keep it short.'

Jorge da Santana went to the bed. 'Riago,' he said quietly, 'you do not need to reply. Just nod, if you understand.' He paused. 'It is about Melanie.'

Melanie, Charlie thought, her heart beating heavily and erratically. The woman they'd both loved, whom Jorge had married. The cause of Riago's isolation here in this wilderness. What about her?

'She has gone, Riago.' Jorge's voice throbbed with emotion. 'She is free once more. I came to tell you this myself—to make amends, if possible, for the wrong I did you.' He took Riago's hand. 'You were right, my brother,' he said with sober intensity. 'She was never mine. Do you understand what I am saying to you?'

There was another silence. Everyone in the room was watching the quiet figure in the bed. Waiting.

Charlie put a hand to her throat. Suddenly it seemed difficult to breathe.

Melanie was free, she thought dazedly. Free, presumably to return to her first love. Free to be with him forever—if that was what he wanted.

And, as if answering her unspoken question as well as his brother's, Riago's head moved on the pillow in a faint but definite nod.

CHAPTER TEN

NO ONE saw Charlie leave the room.

She walked slowly and carefully to her own room. She closed the door behind her, leaned against it and began to shake.

It was over—even before it had begun. That's what she had to face—to come to terms with.

Dignity, she thought. I must behave with dignity.

She could be thankful now that she had never told Riago that she loved him. Grateful, too, that he had no inkling about the baby. There could be no division of his loyalties now, no rekindling of his sense of honour—not now, not when the woman he loved was free to come back into his life.

But for that she would have fought to stay with him, pleaded her case over Philip Hughes—made him understand. Done her best to fill the empty space in his life, even if she would only ever be second-best at most.

But he didn't want her love, so the greatest gift she could give him instead would be the return of his own freedom, without strings.

No protests, she told herself. No more vain attempts to justify herself in his eyes. He'd told her to go, after all. All she had to do was accept that dismissal—and leave.

His self-imposed exile here was coming to an end too. He would be reconciled with his family now, and able to play a full part in its life and business affairs. Live and work where he chose, in fact.

She had no idea what the Brazilian laws were, but she presumed there would be a discreet and amicable divorce. And when the dust had settled he and Melanie would be married. By which time she herself would be long gone...

Melanie. She tasted the name. Not overtly Brazilian, she thought, but then, why should it be? She tried to imagine what the other woman looked like, but no image formed in her mind. She'd have to be beautiful, she thought, to cause such havoc in people's lives.

She, on the other hand, would hardly create a ripple, she thought, staring across the room at the slim, pale, brown-haired reflection she saw in the mirror.

If Riago ever looked back on this time he would see it as a kind of temporary madness, a symptom of the deeper, darker unhappiness which the loss of Melanie had engendered.

She was glad she had the power to make him sane and happy again, even if it was at the expense of her own needs.

It could even be a blessing in disguise. After all, she would never be necessary to Riago in the way she wanted. If she stayed—married him—she would occupy some shadowy position on the edge of his world, never the centre, as she wanted. It was better, healthier in every way to make a clean break.

As for herself, the new life she had thought about before setting off on this adventure had now become a necessity rather than a dream.

She couldn't go home, even if she wanted to, desolate and pregnant, to face the inevitable endless recriminations from her mother and Sonia. She would get an excellent reference from her present employers, so she could seek some kind of residential housekeeping job, where she'd be able to have the baby with her.

How odd, she thought wonderingly, that she was able to stand here and make these plans when she was mentally and emotionally breaking apart. How strange she should look so calm and in control, when inwardly she was screaming—disintegrating.

But a semblance of normality had to be preserved. For the time being she was still required to act as if she was still about to become the mistress of the house.

She would have to find out if their guests were staying or returning to Laragosa immediately. Padre Gaspar almost certainly would be keen to get back to the mission. He probably wouldn't be very pleased to have been sent on a fool's errand in the first place. Jorge da Santana should have warned him, she thought. Given him a much stronger hint about the real purpose of his visit, and saved him a wasted journey. But perhaps Jorge had felt the priest would disapprove, and with good reason. He'd been summoned to conduct a marriage, after all, not to preside over a break-up, and a re-shuffle of the parties involved, no matter how selfless the motive.

She hoped that the visitors wouldn't want to stay, so that she could leave on the boat with them, as Riago had indeed suggested, she recalled with a pang. It would certainly be easier all round if she could just...slip away while he was still sedated. It would obviate the necessity of any awkward last confrontation with him, for one thing, as well as the pain of actually saying goodbye.

She just hoped she could get through it all without breaking down or making a fool of herself in any other way.

I have to learn to be strong, she thought. This is as good a start as any.

A sharp rap on the door startled her.

'Who is it?'

'Afonza, *senhorita*. May I come in?'

The doctor. Her heart skipped a beat as she opened the door. 'Is something wrong? Riago isn't worse?'

'No—no,' he said reassuringly. 'He has had a rough time, but he should make an excellent recovery. No, I came to see you. Just now you looked as if you might faint, and I was concerned.'

She gave an uneven laugh. 'I'm not really the fainting kind.'

'Yet you have been through quite an ordeal, seeing Riago with a gunshot wound. I hear that you also acted as a midwife earlier.' His smile was kind.

She shrugged. 'These things happen.'

'Yes, they do.' His eyes assessed her shrewdly. 'But they do not altogether explain your pallor—

the shadows beneath your eyes.' He put a hand out and gently tipped up her face. 'The bruise on your mouth.' He frowned. 'How did you acquire that?'

'Someone hit me,' she said. 'I think, under the circumstances, I got off lightly.'

He continued to scrutinise her, his frown deepening. He said abruptly, 'Are you certain there is nothing you wish to consult me about?'

'No.' A tinge of guilty colour stole into her face. 'No, nothing, really.'

'Ah,' he said, and paused. 'We have only just met, of course,' he went on, giving her another long look. 'Perhaps over the next few days, *senhorita*, you will come to trust me a little more.' He smiled again and bowed a little. 'We shall meet at dinner, when I hope to have good news of Riago.'

'I hope so too.' She watched him leave, the phrase 'the next few days' still ringing unpleasantly in her ears. That didn't promise an early return to Laragosa, she thought with dismay. Unless the other two were going, leaving just Dr Afonza to look after Riago. She would just have to keep her fingers crossed.

But fortune was not on her side. Dinner that evening soon revealed that all of her guests planned to stay on for an indefinite period, including Padre Gaspar, who explained that he intended to visit the local settlements to perform baptisms.

'I hope we will not be a problem.' Jorge gave her an apologetic look. 'But, you understand, my brother and I have many things to discuss as soon as he is strong enough.'

Charlie cleared her throat. 'Er—when will that be?'

'Sooner than I approve of,' Dr Afonza said drily. 'Riago does not react well to immobility. He even wished to join us for dinner tonight.'

'The miracles that love can do,' Jorge smiled.

Charlie winced inwardly. She supposed that Jorge, along with the rest of Riago's family, knew that his offer of marriage to herself had only been made from a sense of obligation, and therefore saw no particular need to be tactful.

And it was certainly no weirder than the rest of his behaviour, she thought ruefully. What other man could cheerfully assign a wife he was supposed to love to someone else—especially his brother—and after everything that. had happened?

Presumably Jorge too had laid his life at this Melanie's feet and was quite prepared to have it kicked out of the way as a result. Yet he didn't give the impression of being a wimp.

This Melanie must be quite some lady to be able to wield such power over both brothers, Charlie thought with wry pain.

When coffee was finished Dr Afonza got to his feet. 'I am going to see my patient,' he announced. 'Perhaps you would like to accompany me, *senhorita*.'

It was definitely more of a command than a suggestion, so Charlie rose reluctantly.

'You ate nothing,' he said abruptly to her as they walked down the passage towards Riago's room. 'I watched you push the food around your plate. It is not a good thing, especially now.'

Charlie decided it would be more prudent not to enquire into the precise meaning of that last remark. She hurried into speech. 'I...just wasn't hungry. Reaction probably.'

'Perhaps.' He was silent for a moment, then said gently, 'You can confide in me. It is safe, I give you my word.'

'Then there is something I'd like to know,' Charlie said, despising herself. She lifted her chin. 'Have—have you ever seen Melanie da Santana?'

'*Sim.*' He sent her a sideways look. 'Why?'

She shrugged evasively. 'I'd just like to know what she looks like, that's all.'

'If that is all, then it is simple. She has a beautiful face and wonderful body. A tall blonde with a tan from California, and those amazing straight perfect teeth that North American women have.' It was his turn to shrug. 'What more can I say? A fantasy woman, like a film star—every man's dream. And not easy to forget.'

'No,' she said, her throat tightening. 'I gathered that. Thank you.'

'*De nada.*' He sounded almost amused. 'An uncle of mine used to say there are two kind of women in the world—those who break, and those who mend. Melanie da Santana belongs definitely to the first category.'

'I think there's a third, too,' she said quietly. 'Those who are broken themselves.'

It was his turn to shrug. 'Well—maybe my uncle didn't know that many women.'

He opened the door of Riago's room, and motioned her to precede him.

To her astonishment, Riago was standing by the window. He was wearing casual cream cotton trousers, and the upper part of his body was bare, except for the sling that supported his injured arm.

'You ask my advice, and then you ignore it,' Dr Afonza said resignedly. 'I told you to rest.'

'I have a hole in my shoulder,' Riago returned flatly. 'I've rested enough.' He looked at Charlie, and bit his lip. 'Now I have to get on with my life.'

'You'll allow your dressing to be changed, I hope.' Dr Afonza was unruffled. 'I will go and arrange the matter with Rosita.'

The door closed gently behind him.

There was a silence, which Charlie, hot with embarrassment, eventually broke. 'I'm sorry about this,' she said. 'It—it wasn't my idea to come here tonight——'

'I know that,' he cut across her. 'It was mine.' He paused. 'We...have to talk.'

'That's really not necessary,' she said hastily.

'I know that it is,' he said with a touch of grimness. 'I have done you an injustice, Carlotta.'

'Oh, but you haven't. It's all fine—really. You mustn't blame yourself. It's all for the best.'

She knew she was babbling inanely, and Riago stared at her, frowning.

'What are you talking about?' he demanded. 'That Hughes—that *inglês*—he struck you, tried to push you from the truck. He could have killed you. Manoel has been here. He told me everything.'

She grimaced. 'Oh. Well, it was very much my own fault, as you said. I was a fool to go with him. I was just...'

'Desperate?' he supplied, his face bleak. 'Ready to risk your life in order to leave here?'

She looked down at the floor. 'I—I suppose so.'

'Obrigado.'

'I had to do it,' she said in a low voice. She was weeping inside. She couldn't look at him. 'You must see that. You and I—it couldn't work. It was impossible—for all kinds of reasons. And I was quite right, you see.' She took a breath. 'Now everything's turned out for the best—for everyone.'

'You think so?' he asked wearily. 'You and Jorge are more optimistic than I am. I can see enormous problems ahead.'

'But you'll be happy eventually,' she said. 'Surely that will compensate for a lot. You'll have what you want—the life you want.' She found she couldn't actually say Melanie's name. 'Apart from...anything else, you can't have enjoyed being isolated from your family.'

'No, but I would not have chosen this means of being reconciled to them either.' He sighed angrily, bitterly. *'Deus,* what a mess it all is.'

'Well, you'll have one less problem when I go.' She tried to sound matter-of-fact. 'Although I still don't know quite when that will be. Padre Gaspar isn't returning to Laragosa as soon as I'd hoped.'

'You don't have to wait for him,' he said curtly. 'Pedrinho will take you down to Mariasanta, and stay with you until you catch your boat.'

'Obrigada,' Charlie said with a catch in her voice. 'You're ... very kind.'

'No.' He shook his head. The faint smile curving his lips held no amusement whatsoever. 'You and I know better than that, *querida.'* He threw his head back. 'I shall curse myself every day of my life for the way I have treated you. I had hoped, you see, to make amends, to teach you that I can be gentle—but I see now that was foolishness.'

The worst kind of foolishness, she thought achingly. She tried to force an answering smile.

'It—it doesn't matter.'

'It matters to me. Carlotta—I cannot bear for you to go from here hating me.'

'I don't. I never could.'

He held out a hand. 'Come here to me for a moment, *faz favor.'*

She went slowly. I shouldn't be doing this, an inner voice told her, but, dear God, I can't help myself...

She looked up at him gravely. 'I should be going. Dr Afonza will be back soon and you still need to rest.'

'I have the remainder of my life to rest in, but not many more hours to spend with you, *carinha.'* He reached into his pocket. 'I said some harsh things to you yesterday. I regret them. I want to return this to you now, without conditions. It is yours to do with as you wish.'

The diamond blazed in the lamplight as he fastened it round her neck.

'No, Riago.' She tried to pull away. 'I can't take it. Especially now. You must keep it—give it to...someone else.'

He held her. 'No,' he said. 'The diamond belongs to you, and it always will.' His fingers traced, briefly, the line of her throat, then lifted to cup her chin as he studied her bruised mouth.

'That animal did this to you?'

She nodded mutely, silenced, transfixed by his nearness.

He said something swift and savage under his breath. Then, 'Does it hurt you?'

'Sometimes.'

'As when you kissed me yesterday?'

She'd hoped that he'd forgotten about that, or at least that it wouldn't be mentioned. Colour rose in her face.

'A little, yes.'

'Poor little one.' His finger traced with infinite gentleness the curve of her mouth. 'Would it cause you too much pain if I kissed you goodbye?'

Yes, she thought with anguish. But not because of any bruise.

'Don't—please.' She tried to step back as he bent towards her.

'You said you didn't hate me.'

'I don't, believe me. But that doesn't make it right for you to kiss me. You—you belong to someone else. Just...let me go, please.'

'I belong to you, only you don't want me,' Riago said bitterly.

'That's not true.' The words were shocked out of her.

'Then what is it? This place? We don't have to live here, not if you don't want. There are other estates, other properties not so remote, more civilised. You can choose, *querida*, only don't leave me.'

'What am I supposed to do?' She faced him furiously. 'Share you with Melanie? I can't. I won't.'

'Melanie?' His brows shot up as he repeated the name incredulously. 'What does that bitch have to do with us?'

'You're in love with her.'

'I was infatuated with her—once. Until she married Jorge. And do you know why she married him? Because she assumed that, as the eldest of my parents' children, he would inherit the bulk of my father's estate.'

'And that's why she threw you over?' Charlie shook her head. 'You must be wrong. She couldn't have done such a thing.'

'I had it from her own lips,' he said drily. 'She expressed regret, of course, but, as the eldest, she told me, Jorge had to be the better catch, even though he wouldn't make as exciting a husband.'

'But if she loved you . . .'

'Love had nothing to do with it. There were two things in Melanie's life—sex and money. And she was prepared to use one with complete ruthlessness to obtain the other.' He smiled grimly. 'But her greed misled her. When Papa died he left everything equally divided between Jorge, Isabella and myself, as is the custom. It was a great and unpleasant shock to Melanie—to find she had sacrificed herself to a man she didn't want for no reason.'

'You didn't warn her it would be like that?'

'Of course not. She was worthless and mercenary. She deserved to be made a fool of.' He paused. 'Instead I tried to warn Jorge, but he was crazy about her, and refused to listen. He'd always been shy with women, not too experienced, and Melanie had gone after him, taken him by storm.'

Charlie swallowed. 'But she took you by storm as well. You told me yourself—all that she meant to you.'

He moved his uninjured shoulder wearily. 'Once, yes. I admit it. She was an exciting woman. But then I saw what she also was, and excitement was replaced by disgust.'

'But it wasn't that simple. Even though you knew what she was, you still wanted her. You know you did.'

'What makes you say that?' he asked sharply. 'What stories have you heard?'

She flushed slightly. 'That, even when she was married to your brother, you still wanted to be her lover. That he...he found you together.'

'Ah, yes,' Riago said softly. 'That much is true, but nothing else. That we should become lovers again was Melanie's idea alone. I had finished with her completely, but I had to go home to discuss some legal matter over Papa's will, and she came to my room—offered herself. She was bored with Jorge, she said.' His face hardened. 'When I refused her she called me a string of foul

names, then she tore her clothes and started
screaming. When Jorge came—and my mother—
she said I had tricked her into being alone with
me, and then tried to rape her.'

He groaned softly. 'Jorge was half mad with
anger and jealousy. I tried to reason with him,
but it was useless. So, as I was due to come here
and work on the rubber project anyway, I just
left. I knew that one day he would find out the
truth about her as I had done. And now, sure
enough, she has left him, gone off with another
man—a Texas oil millionaire, I understand. I
wish him luck.'

She drew a desperate breath. 'But, no matter
what she's done, you must still care a little. You
told me so yourself in this very room. You said
you'd met the woman you'd love all your life,
but that she didn't want you.'

'I remember it perfectly,' he said. 'Only,
carinha, I wasn't talking about Melanie.' He
touched the curve of her cheek with his hand. 'I
meant you.'

'No,' she said unevenly. 'That—can't be.'

'Why not?' His face, his voice were stark—
sombre. 'You don't think I'm capable of finding
real love at last? Because I made a mistake with
Melanie, must I be condemned to loneliness for
ever after?'

'But you don't love me. You can't.' Her heart
was hammering so violently that she felt almost
stifled. 'I'm not even pretty,' she added wildly.

'You are beautiful,' he said. 'You have brought
gentleness and grace to my home, and my life.'

'You hardly know me.' Her voice wavered.

'You think love cannot happen in so short a time.' Riago shook his head. 'You are wrong, *carinha*. I think I have always known you—always been waiting for you.' His tone deepened passionately. 'I'd hoped that you might, one day, come to feel the same about me. But I suppose it is impossible. Too much has happened too soon for you to trust me. I don't blame you. After all, you have never pretended to care for me. And you have a life of your own back in England.'

She looked up at him gravely, her heart in her eyes. 'I have an existence.'

It was his turn to draw a sharp breath. 'What are you trying to say?'

She tried to smile. 'That, with love, anything is possible—even in a very short time.'

'You truly love me?' His voice was tender, but it held a note that sent all her pulses crazy.

'More than any life anywhere.' She flung her head back. 'I want to stay with you, Riago. I want to be your wife.'

'I've dreamed of this,' he said huskily. 'Of hearing you say those words, night after night in this cursed bed, alone. Tell me I'm not dreaming now.' For the first time he sounded diffident, almost vulnerable, and her heart cracked with answering tenderness and delight.

She went into the circle of his uninjured arm, and lifted her face to his. 'Will this convince you?' she asked softly, then their lips touched, clung in a fusion too deep and too sweet for further words.

When at last they drew apart Riago stroked back her hair, giving an unsteady laugh. 'My bride,' he murmured. 'My love. How you fought against me.'

Charlie shook her head. 'I was fighting myself, I think,' she said softly.

'And now is it peace between us?'

She smiled up at him, lovingly, teasingly. 'Oh, there'll be other battles, I don't doubt. You can be quite an autocrat.'

'And yet you will still take the risk?'

'I'll risk anything.' She rested her cheek against his chest, knowing that, for her, all the safety and security the world had to offer lay in his arms. 'Every day an adventure.'

She reached up to kiss him again, smiling against his lips as she thought of the baby.

The first wonderful adventure of their lives together had already begun.

'Darling——' Happiness lilted in her voice. 'I've got something to tell you.'

HARLEQUIN ✿ PRESENTS®

A Year
DOWN UNDER

In 1993, Harlequin Presents celebrates the land down under. In May, let us take you to Auckland, New Zealand, in SECRET ADMIRER by Susan Napier, Harlequin Presents #1554.

Scott Gregory is ready to make his move. He's realized Grace is a novice at business *and* emotionally vulnerable— a young widow struggling to save her late husband's company. But Grace is a fighter. She's taking business courses and she's determined not to forget Scott's reputation as a womanizer. Even if it means adding another battle to the war—a fight against her growing attraction to the handsome New Zealander!

Share the adventure—and the romance— of A Year Down Under!

Available this month in
A YEAR DOWN UNDER

A DANGEROUS LOVER
by Lindsay Armstrong
Harlequin Presents #1546
Wherever Harlequin books are sold.

YDU-A

Following the success of WITH THIS RING and
TO HAVE AND TO HOLD, Harlequin brings you

JUST MARRIED

SANDRA CANFIELD
MURIEL JENSEN
ELISE TITLE
REBECCA WINTERS

just in time for the 1993 wedding season!

Written by four of Harlequin's most popular authors, this
four-story collection celebrates the joy, excitement and
adjustment that comes with being "just married."

You won't want to miss this spring tradition, whether
you're just married or not!

AVAILABLE IN APRIL WHEREVER HARLEQUIN
BOOKS ARE SOLD

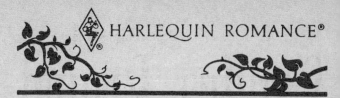

HARLEQUIN SUPERROMANCE®

HARLEQUIN SUPERROMANCE NOVELS WANTS TO INTRODUCE YOU TO A DARING NEW CONCEPT IN ROMANCE...

WOMEN WHO DARE!
Bright, bold, beautiful...
Brave and caring, strong and passionate...
They're women who know their own minds
and will dare anything...
for love!

One title per month in 1993, written by popular Superromance authors, will highlight our special heroines as they face unusual, challenging and sometimes dangerous situations.

Next month, time and love collide in:
#549 PARADOX by Lynn Erickson
Available in May wherever Harlequin Superromance novels are sold.

If you missed any of the Women Who Dare titles and would like to order them, send your name, address, zip or postal code along with a check or money order for $3.39 for each book ordered (do not send cash), plus 75¢ ($1.00 in Canada) for postage and handling, payable to Harlequin Reader Service, to:

In the U.S.	In Canada
3010 Walden Avenue	P.O. Box 609
P.O. Box 1325	Fort Erie, Ontario
Buffalo, NY 14269-1325	L2A 5X3

Please specify book title(s) with your order.
Canadian residents add applicable federal and provincial taxes.

WWD-MY

Where do you find hot Texas nights, smooth Texas charm and dangerously sexy cowboys?

AMARILLO BY MORNING

Show time—Texas style!

Everybody loves a cowboy, and Cal McKinney is one of the best. So when designer Serena Davis approaches this handsome rodeo star, the last thing Cal expects is a business proposition!

CRYSTAL CREEK reverberates with the exciting rhythm of Texas. Each story features the rugged individuals who live and love in the Lone Star State. And each one ends with the same invitation...

Y'ALL COME BACK...REAL SOON!

Don't miss *AMARILLO BY MORNING* by Bethany Campbell. Available in May wherever Harlequin books are sold.
